THE DEVIL'S BELT

ERIC MORENO

For my beautiful and supportive wife, Valentina,
whose love gives me strength,
and for my son, Leandro,
soon to arrive and already so deeply loved.

Eric Moreno
The Devil's Belt

ISBN: 978-1-7331100-2-0
Printed in the United States of America

A couple in their early twenties peered through the storefront window of an antique shop. The smudged glass had large gold lettering in old English font that read Ye Olde Antiques. "Come on," the young girl said fogging up the window. She eagerly pulled on her boyfriend's hand as she led him in. A golden doorbell that hung above the entry rang as they stepped inside the oddly dim shop, brightened by two golden Victorian table lamps placed on the floor toward the back by the furniture area. Sunlight shined through the large window illuminating the front area. The peculiar store was filled with vintage dusty wooden furniture that smelled of must and strong hints of wood polish. The back of the store was cluttered with old vintage cushioned chairs stacked on top of each other and sofa's that looked as if they hadn't been sat on in decades. To the left of the shop were two long racks of clothing that had a pungent odor of mothballs. On the right was a long glass countertop display case holding an eye-catching old-fashioned brass cash register. The white walls were adorned with 19th century black and white photos of people in curious poses and golden framed landscape paintings. Crystal chandeliers and ornate oil lamps hung from the ceiling.

"Wow, look at all this cool stuff," Lilith said as she stared in amazement. Her boyfriend Michael Adler looked around incuriously as Lilith browsed the store.

"Looking for anything in particular?" Michael asked, crouched gazing at a medieval Gargoyle sculpture. The Gargoyle's bulging eyes, and long fangs held Michael's attention before looking up at Lilith who stood in front of him holding a black leather belt.

"Look, I found you this. It has animal designs on it. Try it on," she said handing him the secondhand belt.

"But I don't need one," Michael said examining it with disinterest. "The one I have is fine, besides I hardly use it anyhow."

Lilith grabbed it and wrapped it around his slim waist, "it fits you perfectly," she said with a radiant smile. "It's better than the one you have now," dismissing his rejection, "which is too long. I just don't see a price tag on it though. Ask the shopkeeper how much."

Michael scoffed. It made no sense for him to ask for the price of an item that he had no interest in, but to appease his girlfriend he languidly walked up to the glass countertop with belt in hand. "Hello?" Michael said out loud looking for someone to assist. He looked to his right and then left. "Is anyone here?"

Just as he opened his mouth to speak louder, a withering old man with fuzzy gray hair stepped out of the shadow from the corner behind the countertop.

"Oh, hello," Michael said with a startled look. "Sorry, I didn't see you there."

"But I saw *you*," the old man replied in a low hoarse voice; the shadow still covering his face. His stony black eyes peered into Michael's mystified brown eyes as he leaned in closer. Michael awkwardly pulled his head back away from the old man who was invading his personal space and placed the belt on the countertop. "How much for the belt?" he asked with a strange and uncomfortable look.

"How much are you willing to pay?" softly replied the old man.

"Well doesn't it have a price?"

"There is a price to pay. But are you willing to pay that price? You see, this is not a regular kind of belt, Michael," said the old man in an ill-boding tone.

"Have we met before? Because I don't remember telling you my name."

"We have," affirmed the old man. With a long pause, he held the belt up with both hands as if holding a sacred object. Michael looked at the old man with a bewildered expression as he stared at his thick bushy eyebrows then down at his mummifying hands and long sharp fingernails. "I know what you want Michael," the old man melodiously said with a wrinkled smile that revealed his rotten yellow teeth. "What you really want. Better than you do. You lust for the sweet taste of blood." He passed his tongue filled with sores across his dry cracked lips as he said it. Michael deeply stared at the old man, hypnotized by his foreboding words. "Wearing this belt can help fulfill those nefarious and morbid desires, the one's you carry around like luggage locked inside that cruel black heart of yours. The one's you try to bury deep within. The one's scratching and clawing their way out. Wear this and let them be free."

Michael stood there quiet, with an elevated heartbeat, gazing intently into the old man's piercing eyes. He studied them as if looking for an answer that would reveal everything about the wicked old man. Darkness coldly stared back at him.

"But you already know who I am, don't you?" asked the old man inching his bulbous nose closer. Michael grew puzzled by the man's ability to read his mind. The old man leaned against the counter, resting his elbows and spoke in an ominous tone, "many moons ago, in the darkness of the night, you came to me," he recalled, "requesting from me that at your pleasure, you might work your malice on men, women and children, in the shape of some beast whereby you may live without dread or danger of life and unknown to be the executer of any bloody endeavor which you meant to commit. And as I did then, I grant you now this magical belt that when worn will transform you into the likeness of a greedy, devouring wolf. In exchange for your soul and eternal servitude during the remainder of your mortal life."

Michael's eyes filled with dread as he fixed his eyes on the belt concentrating on the animal designs which he now could make out to be those of a wolf. He then felt a burning sensation grow inside the pit of his stomach that spread to his lower back like a massive wildfire that made him wince. He slowly took a step back holding his stomach, never taking his eyes off the old man as he reached for the door.

"You're a crazy old fool with wild shit stories and your breath smells twice as bad. So bad, that it makes me nauseas. I've never seen you in my life before today and you know nothing about me," Michael sternly said.

"Sie sind Peter Stumpp, der werewolf von Bedburg, der das fleisch von frauen und kindern verschlingt!" the old man loudly growled in German language.

Michael swallowed the lump in his throat. "Lilith!" he shouted standing by the door, "let's go." He stared at the old man with a disturbed look. The old man waved the belt at him with a baleful glare. Michael flung the door open as Lilith quickly sorted through the clothing rack. "Lilith!" Michael shouted once more.

"Okay, coming," she retorted speedily walking toward the door.

"Excuse me young lady," the old man said waving his hand at her. "Your boyfriend forgot this." He held the belt out in front of him and dangled it in the air.

"Oh, gosh thank you," Lilith said as she hurried to the counter.

"No, thank you," replied the old man with a pleasant grin.

Michael impatiently waited outside pacing back and forth. "How much was it?" Lilith asked handing him the belt.

"What the hell?" Michael asked angrily. "Take it back. I don't want it."

"But he handed it to me to give to you," Lilith replied with a perplexing look. Michael snatched the belt from her hand and stormed back to the door. "I didn't pay for it because I don't want it," he irately stated. He pulled on the door handle and found it locked. He pulled again harder, back and forth but still the door remained shut. The lights were off and the old shopkeeper was nowhere to be seen.

"Looks like he's closed it down now," Lilith said shielding her eyes peeking through the glass. Michael banged on the door with his fist and pulled on the door handle. He looked through the window searching for the old man and used the belt's metal buckle to furiously tap on the glass. The store was completely dark and quiet. Michael scanned the glass counter area but couldn't see a thing. "Let's just go," Lilith said and grabbed Michael by the hand. They made a short walk back to her car that was parked a few parking meters down from the store. Lilith unlocked the doors with her key fob and Michael turned to stare one last time at the antique store. She stood at the driver's side and grabbed the door handle, momentarily pausing at seeing Michael fixated on the window. She opened the door, placed her purse in the back seat and turned the key to start the engine. "Coming?" she asked looking up at Michael through the passenger window as she fastened her seatbelt. "He didn't come out," Michael said with a strange look as he got in the car. "What do you mean?" Lilith asked staring back. "I didn't see him come out of the store. And there's no parking in the back. So, where did he go?"

"Maybe he goes out the back and walks home?"

"No, he looked way too old to walk home."

"Then maybe he sleeps there? A lot of business owners sleep in their place of business to avoid paying additional rent or a mortgage."

"Yeah, maybe. Rude of him not to answer me though when I was banging on the door."

"Maybe the poor old man was in the restroom changing his diaper?"

"Yeah," Michael said with a chuckle. "Maybe."

During the drive to Lilith's apartment in the city of Santa Monica, Michael quietly sat in the passenger seat looking out the window staring off into space. The leather belt was set on the floor in between his feet. Lilith steered the wheel, occasionally glancing over at him. The radio played an ad for auto insurance and the ventilation system blew in warm air from the cranked-up heater. The day turned unusually cold, although the weather forecast predicted a nice warm day in the mid-seventies. As Lilith eased off the gas pedal, she turned to look at Michael again and could tell that he was bothered. The ride back to her place had been quiet for the most part, except for her failed attempts at sparking a conversation. She felt that perhaps his gloomy mood was caused by something she may have said or done. She knew herself well to know that at times, and without realizing it, she could come be demeaning or come off as mean by saying an offensive comment. Like the time when she politely told a customer at the clothing store of where she works that they didn't sell clothing for women who were expecting, but at the other end of the mall was a store with an entire section for pregnant women. The hefty woman with short blonde hair was infuriated and angrily told her with a heavy breath that she wasn't pregnant and stormed out. Lilith was unsure of how to approach the situation with Michael and wasn't looking to start a fight. As traffic slowed on the congested freeway, she lowered the radio and placed her hand on his knee. "What's wrong?" she finally asked.

"Nothing," he answered tersely.

"Is it about the belt?" she asked switching her attention between him and the road.

"No," he answered looking down at the belt in between his dirty white sneakers.

"Did I do something? Or say something wrong?"

"No," Michael replied adjusting in his seat.

"You've just been really quiet since we left the store and I don't know if I said or did something to bother you," Lilith said easing off the brake.

"It's not you, it's that creepy old man from the store. Something about him and all the crazy things he said ... I don't know, kind of weirded me out. Especially something he said in German."

"He spoke in German to you?" Lilith asked with a laugh. "What did he say?"

"That's the thing, I know what he said, but I don't know, if that makes any sense," Michael said with a confused look.

"Yeah, no, it doesn't," Lilith replied with an apologetic smile.

"When he spoke to me, I felt like I knew what he said at that precise moment which really upset me, but I can't remember what he said. And even if I did, I have no clue of what it means in English. Yet I feel uneasy about it."

Lilith turned her signal to merge lanes and checked the passenger mirror. "What were some of the other things that he said that bothered you?" she asked while turning the wheel. Michael shook his head and stared out the window, watching as cars passed by. "Nothing," he said. "It's dumb anyway."

She reached for his hand and felt his cold palm press against hers as they locked fingers. Her thumb caressed against his. As he studied her black fingernails, Lilith could sense that he brooded over the old man's words. An upbeat song that he liked began to play on the radio. She turned up the volume in hopes of lifting his spirits. It was the number one song on the billboard charts for the third week straight and was on constant rotation. She bopped her head along to the beat and hummed the lyrics while shaking his hand to the rhythm of the song. He cracked a smile and jokily bopped his head to the beat with her.

At her apartment, Lilith laid her purse on the kitchen counter and opened the refrigerator to grab a bottle of water and asked if he wanted something to drink. Michael sat on the sofa and shook his head. He had a concentrated look, staring in a disconcerting way at the black leather belt he placed on top of the round glass coffee table. "A beer or anything?" Lilith asked standing by the sink that overflowed with dirty dishes. "No, I'm good, thanks," he replied combing his fingers through his shaggy hair. She walked over to the living room while taking a sip of water and stood in front of him. He looked her up and stared into her enthralling green eyes with dark eye shadow and winged eyeliner. Her eyes moved away from his pointy chin to fixate on the rest of his body. She set the bottle down on the table and stepped closer. She lightly pushed him against the sofa and raised her leg over his knee to sit on top of him. "What's wrong?" she softly asked caressing his face. He held her by the waist and looked at her dark red lips shying away from her fervid eyes and shook his head. She licked her heart shaped lips and gave him a gentle kiss. Her arms wrapped around his neck as she massaged his lips with her tongue engaging in an ardently kiss. His fingers ran through her soft black hair as their tongues swirled around one another's like a pair of ballet dancers. His hands came down to caress her back before gradually sliding down to her butt. He lifted her up and gently brought her down on the sofa. She spread her legs open and unbuttoned her shorts. Michael stood up looking down at her, "I'm sorry," he said regretfully. "I'm just not in the mood right now. I have a lot on my mind and I think it's best if I go home and call it a day." He grabbed his keys and belt off the coffee table and proceeded for the door. "I'll text you when I'm home," he said standing in the doorway. She waved from the sofa as he walked out. Once she heard his footsteps fading out in the hallway, she got up and walked to the kitchen to grab a lighter from her purse. She lit a large yellow vanilla scented candle that was set on top of the coffee table, placed a sofa pillow against the armrest and laid down conformably with her head rested on the pillow. The scent of vanilla permeated the small living room as the heat of the flame melted the wax. Lilith took in a deep breath followed by a long exhale and closed her eyes.

It was a troubling night for Michael. Sleep had eluded him. He spent the last couple of hours tossing and turning in his bed, unable to sleep. He laid on his side, wrapped up in a soft warm blanket with his eyes closed toiling to remain shut. Once again, he made another attempt at gaining sleep by clearing his mind of all thoughts and pictured himself in a void space; enclosed by darkness with nothing and no one in it. He inhaled deeply and slowly exhaled through his nose. His abdomen raised and fell with each breath. With his body now relaxed, he felt himself slowly falling into deep slumber until the faint sound of feet loudly dragging through dark woke him. Michael's breathing grew faster with every irking footstep. A light flickered revealing the old man leaning on a glass counter. He stood cold and quiet. The old man's eerie silence petrified Michael who was now standing across from him. The old man then cackled with laughter, deriding Michael. Anger set upon Michael's face who muffled loudly in an attempt to yell. His eyes shot open waking him from the nightmare. His forehead damp with sweat. He huffed in frustration as he lay awake, and thought of the old man, grimly standing behind the counter. He envisioned the black leather belt fully laid out on the counter and the old man wickedly grinning. Michael turned to lay on his back and stared up at the dark celling. He stretched his hand out to the night stand next to his bed, picked up his phone and checked the time. *Fuck an hour?* he thought to himself, looking at the phone with displeasure. It was a quarter past three. He placed the phone back down and squeezed his eyes shut once again and entered the void. This time, he tried a breathing technique which helps to fall asleep, one that Michael learned about through one of his friends who was studying to be a therapist. Their conversation took place in a crowded burger stand as Michael would recollect. The long line of people stretched out the door as they waited their turn to place an order. As the two friends sat at a small white round table and ate their burger, Michael's longtime high school friend shared the technique he learned from a class he took during the fall semester. He dipped a handful of fries into the small ketchup cup container as he chewed and held the greasy cheese burger with the other hand. Michael sipped from the straw and listened. Step one, take a deep and long breath in. Michael inhaled deeply through his nose again, feeling the cool air fill his lungs. Step two, exhale completely and focus on how it makes your body feel. Michael pushed the air out from his lungs, feeling his abdomen drop. Step three, after doing the first and second steps for a couple of times, your exhale should last twice as long as your inhale. Michael followed the steps as he laid in bed, slowly exhaling. The tranquility that he yearned for finally come over him and he felt relaxed. Peter, he heard softly whispered into his ear. Michael's eyes opened wide with terror at feeling someone's hot breath flow through his ear canal. He lifted his head to look around the dark room, faintly lit with the illumination of the bright full moon shining through the bedroom window across the bed. What he saw was the forty-inch television directly in front of him set on top of the wooden drawer next to the window. He then stared at the half open closet door. He glanced over at the pile of dirty clothes thrown on top of his timeworn desk chair. No one else was in the room. He slowly laid his head back down on the pillow with his eyes alert examining the room from corner to corner. *That was weird.* He chalked it up to his wild imagination running freely. *Focus. Focus.* He turned to his other side and pulled the blanket up to his neck to keep warm, sheltering both feet inside. He took a deep breath and went back into the void. *Keep focusing.* A minute passed as he concentrated, waiting to go through all stages of sleep, REM sleep, an acronym for rapid eye movement, being the reward for a frustrating sleepless night. Peter Stumpp! he heard called out, in a loud and raging voice. He threw the blanket off and sprang out of bed. His feet pitter-pattered across the wooden floor as he dashed for the light switch next to the bedroom door. Once he flicked the light switch, he quickly turned around and pushed his back against the door. Fear had set upon his face, his eyes wide and filled with dread studied the room from wall to wall. It was quiet, except for the crickets chirping outside of his bedroom window and the sound of a vehicle driving off in the distance. Finding the room empty, he turned to his right and yanked the closet door open with haste. He stepped in tugging at the pull chain above him which turned the light on. He promptly flipped through the hung clothes, parting shirts and hangers out of the way to inspect the back wall. There was no one there. He glimpsed up at his shoe boxes neatly stacked on top of the shelf just as he had left them, then looked down at his closet storage units. Everything was in its place. He turned around and looked at his bedroom again, directing his attention down at the bottom of the bed. His eyes intensely shifted to the floor underneath the bedframe. With nerves flaring and palms sweating, he tiptoed to the bed. He wiped his palms against his sleep shorts and slowly dropped to a knee to take a look. His temple pressed against the floor and he swiftly lifted the sheets up over the bed. Dirty pairs of sneakers and empty shoe boxes covered in dust were scattered beneath the bed. Beside one of the shoes boxes was the black leather belt neatly rolled up. Michael had tossed it underneath the bed when he got home earlier that evening and left it there to forget about. He pulled the sheets down as he stood up and curiously turned his head to the closet then back to the other side of the room trying to make sense of the voice he clearly heard. *Hmm.* His eyebrows drew together in a confused look as he walked back to the light switch. He brought his hand up to the switch and paused momentarily before turning it off to take another look at his room. He sighed and turned the lights off, then swiftly turned them back on as if waiting for someone or something to suddenly appear before him. *I'm losing it.* The room went dark once the lights turned off again and he crawled back under the blanket pulling it over his chest. He laid flat on his back with his hand over his rib cage as he looked up at the ceiling trying to make sense of what he heard. As he grew deeper in thought, his eyelids began to weigh heavy. Sleep that he desperately sought began to finally take over and his body was at ease. There were less distractions floating around in his head, his breathing grew steady and anxiety levels dropped. His eyes twitched the deeper he went into sleep. As the night progressed, Michael murmured in his sleep. Sweat dripped from his forehead and a look of anguish settled on his face. Wheezing sounds followed like a person who suffered from asthma. He squinted his face and let out another murmur while holding his belly. The low murmurs had turned into louder wails. He clenched his fist in pain. By now his breathing had grown faster and sweat was steadily trickling out the pores. Flashing images of gurgling blood dribbling down prodigiously long fangs that gleamed under the moon rushed through his mind. Sweat flowed down the side of his head and dripped onto the pillow. His eyes rapidly darted about as he dreamt. The combination of a woman's terrifying shrieks that echoed through the cold night and sounds of a wild animal savagely snarling as it tore apart its prey rang through his head like a thunderous clang. The top of the blanket covering his chest was soaked with sweat. The sheets dragged out from the corner of the bed with his kicking and uncontrollable leg jerk. During the incessant nightmare, he visualized a woman's fingers frenetically clawing into the earth while pinned down by an enormous hairy beast with glowing red eyes filled with rage. Grass blades caressed in between her thin fingers. Dirt quickly packed under her fingernails. A patch of grass was yanked from the soil. As the beast fed on her mutilated body, her fingers slowly lost motion. Blood spots splattered onto her lifeless hand. Michael's scrunched up face glistened with sweat. His lips twitched wanting to speak and after a few lip quivers he muttered a few words. As the nightmare kept up, the image of the old man standing in complete darkness holding out the leather belt with both hands came to mind again. A single dim light illumed over the old man's deteriorating face as he opened his cracked lips to speak, Sie sind Peter Stumpp, der Werewolf von Bedburg, der das fleisch von fraun und kindern verschlingt. The old man released the belt and let it drop by Michael's white sneakers. The withering old man slowly stepped out of the light back into darkness and softly repeated in English, "You are Peter Stumpp, the Werewolf of Bedburg, who gorges on the flesh of women and children."

The next morning, Michael was in the kitchen yawning as he fixed himself a bowl of cereal. The cereal crackled as milk poured over it filling the bowl halfway. He put the lid on the milk carton and placed it back in the refrigerator. He picked up the bowl from the kitchen counter and set it down on the kitchen table. He huffed as he pulled out the wooden chair to take a seat. His eyes were red and swollen from a lack of sleep. The spoon scraped against the bowl as he scooped up the cereal swimming in milk.

At that moment, Elisa, Michael's older sister walked into the kitchen and opened the refrigerator door. "Morning Peter Stumpp," she said as she grabbed the milk. The spoon dropped and settled against the bowl as Michael stared up at her most intently. "What did you call me?"

he asked with wide troubling eyes. "That's what you said last night, in your sleep," Elisa replied tipping the box of cereal into the bowl. "I came home like at three a.m. tip toeing to my room trying not to wake mom and dad, but your ass screamed out something in German that I couldn't understand, except for Peter Stumpp. You might as well have made a public announcement or rang an alarm to let them know that I got home late."

Michael looked down at his soggy cereal in confusion. "I don't remember that," he said playing with the spoon parting the cereal.

"I haven't heard you speak in German since you were like five."

"What are you talking about?" Michael questioned with a disturbed look in his eye.

She took a seat at the table and sat across from him. Her hair was frizzy and in a pony tail which she tossed to her back. Michael anxiously waited for her response and watched as she brought the spoonful of cereal to her mouth. The cereal crunched as she chewed. She reached for a napkin at the center of the table to wipe the milk from her lips. Michael kept his eyes on her patiently waiting for her to answer. "When you were four, you used to talk in German," she finally answered. "Not very well, but you could say like a full-on sentence, which was strange to us for obvious reasons, none of us speak German. We're not even German. Mom and Dad had a teacher's conference at your preschool and even they couldn't explain how you were able to speak the language. None of your little classmates spoke the language, not the teacher herself, the teacher's aide, not even the principal." Michael listened attentively. He felt a rush of blood shoot over his face as the weight of emotions came down on him.

"What were some of the things I would say?" he frightenedly asked, afraid of the response.

"Well after we found a translator, a friend of one of dad's friends, we learned that you would say you were a man who lived in a town in Germany and that you were a very bad man. You said you used to be hairy and tall with big teeth, then you growled. It was the cutest thing. In fact,

I think you said the town's name last night in your sleep. Burg or bodrug or bedbug," she said trying to recall.

"Bedburg," he replied somberly.

"Yeah," she said enthusiastically. "See you do remember."

Michael looked discomposed, mentally processing all his sister had said. He had no memory of it. Questions of his childhood danced all around his head. One after the other like pounding rain flooding his mind. Why couldn't he remember some of it? Had he completely forgotten all about it or had he intentionally suppressed his memories? Was there a connection with the old man in any of this? He pondered while drooped in the chair with an elbow on the table and face rested on his hand. A feeling of sadness and confusion coated his face which his sister could read. After several years of seeing her little brother grow up and learning all of the emotions his face would wear, she knew this wretched look had to do with the bombshell of a story she unintentionally set off. Milk dripped from beneath the spoon as she brought a spoonful of cereal up to her mouth. "Is there anything else that about my childhood that was, I guess kind of weird?"

"Mhm," she uttered, with a nod of her head. The cereal crunched loudly as she quickly chewed to spew the words out. She brought her hand up to cover her mouth as she began to speak. "I remember once, and I think you were five at this time, just before you completely stopped speaking in German, you said something about a belt." Michaels eyes grew wide as he listened intently to the story. He laid his hands down flat on the table as he leaned in closer. "What about the belt?" he asked tensely. Elisa wiped her mouth again with the same crumpled up napkin. "You'd say, 'I get my super powers from a belt that a man gave me and every time I wear the belt, I become stronger like a wolf with long sharp claws', and you went on and on about how strong you were and that you would scare everyone in this town and do very bad things. You never explained exactly what you did, but you said people would scream really loud whenever you touched them. Especially the babies." At that moment, Michael's face lost all shade of color and for a second, his breath got stuck in the back of his throat. He pushed himself away from the table and hurried out of the kitchen. He ran up the stairs to his room quickly locking the door behind him. He grabbed the laptop from underneath the pile of clothes on the chair and sat on the bed with it. As the laptop powered on, his heart raced, and his feet got hot from the blood that circulated through his toes. Anxiety began to settle in once the home screen came on. His stomach started churning and his breathes were shorter. He opened a web browser and typed in Peter Stumpp. The search results found a link to the true story of Peter Stumpp, the Bedburg serial killer, He clicked the link and swallowed the lump he had stuck in his throat. As the page opened, he quickly breezed through the article, reading as quickly as his eyes could follow each word. There were several shocking words that stood out like German serial killer, accused of werewolfery, cannibalism, pact with the devil. For the next two hours, he surfed the web, reading articles and watching videos of the man he heard called out in his dreams. An article from the history facts website read:

There is historical evidence to support the following: In 1589 Peter Stumpp, the Werewolf of Bedburg, faced one of the most famous werewolf trials in history. He was arrested for committing a string of heinous murders in the small German town of Bedburg. While stretched on a rack and under heavy torture, he confessed to having practiced black magic since the age of twelve. Stumpp claimed that the Devil had given him a magical belt that enabled him to metamorphose into a wolf. He confessed to having killed 16 people, thirteen of them children, two men and two pregnant women, whose fetuses he ripped from their wombs and ate their hearts "panting hot and raw" which he later described as "dainty morsels." One of the thirteen children was his own son, whose brains he was reported to have devoured. He would sexually assault young women before tearing them apart. Small children were strangled to death, bludgeoned, and throats ripped open. Some were disemboweled and partially eaten. Among the accusations, Stumpp was also accused of having an incestuous relationship with his own daughter, who bore him the son that he killed.

As he read bits of new information, shrills of fear coursed through his veins propping up the hairs on his arm like a strong breeze blowing through a field of tall grass. Flashes of vivid heinous crimes popped in his head. He visualized everything that would have transpired so clearly, that he could see the most minute details such as the color of the victim's hair or the garment that they wore just before getting tattered and drenched in blood. He could smell fear reeking from the victim. It was intoxicating and he lusted for more. He was unnerved by these sudden visions and senses that were all too real. He clicked on another video. He impatiently huffed as the spinning circle rotated as the page loaded. The video played and the narrator with a low ghostly voice gave more or less of the of the same information as the other ones. He wanted more information. Accounts of what the devil may have looked like or anything that would mention the pact that was made with the devil. That's when he placed the laptop down by his pillow and sprang out of bed. He rushed to his sister's bedroom across from his and banged on the door. Elisa cracked the door open, wearing a white towel wrapped around her body. Her hair dripping with water from having stepped out of the shower. "What the heck's your problem?" she demanded standing by the door with an angry look on her face.

"Did I ever say what the man looked like? The man who gave me the belt?"

"What?" asked Elisa with an agitated and confused look.

"When I was kid, did I ever give any details about what the man who gave me the belt may have looked like?"

"No," she replied holding a bewildered look. Michael looked down in discontent.

"But you drew him," Elisa said. "You drew a lot when you were a kid and I think he's in one of your drawings."

"Where's that drawing?"

"In the garage. Mom boxed up all our stuff from when we were kids. Yours should be labeled Mikey."

Before Michael could walk away in a hurry, she stopped him. "What's this all about Michael?" she asked with a concerned look standing by the doorway. He shook his head suggesting that nothing was wrong. Michael darted for the stairs. His hand slid down the wooden rail as he quickly got down the stairs, jumping three steps and another three until his feet landed with a boom causing a loud thump. Had his mother been home she surely would have yelled at him to walk down the stairs like a normal person as she's often yelled out before. He turned the hall decorated with family portraits. One of Michael age six and his sister aged ten both posing with their arms around one another and a smile from ear to ear. Michael opened the door that led to the garage and hit the light switch. He maneuvered his way through camping gear, bicycles, plastic storage totes, and an old but comfortable leather recliner covered up in plastic that his dad had a hard time letting go of. Toward the corner were piles of boxes labeled x-mas ornaments that were stacked on top of thanksgiving ornaments which were stacked on top of Halloween ornaments. He shoved and pushed them aside wiggling his way toward the back where he found the box labeled Mikey. To make room, he pushed the ornament boxes a bit further out and pulled the two boxes down. He undid the tape and dug through his box, pulling out awards and certificates from his time in elementary. He found manila folders containing graded papers and report cards and set a pile of the things he pulled out. He opened another manila folder and found colored drawings. He sat on the dusty floor and crossed his legs holding the folder. He flipped through the drawings. Some were of a sun shining over a beach with a boat. Another of a black dog with red eyes. Another drawing was of his family standing in front of their home. He had labeled each family member with their title above their head. There was Mom and Dad, Sister and Me.

Another drawing was of a green dinosaur with several sharp teeth. The next drawing was of a man with frizzy white hair. His eyes were colored in completely black, and his skin was outlined with wrinkles. His fingernails were long. He wore black clothes and black shoes. Next to his foot was what appeared to be a long black snake. Michael held the drawing up closer to his face and realized that it was a belt. He was staring at a drawing he made long ago of the old man from the antique store.

Chapter 3

It was one in the afternoon and Lilith was growing impatient. She huffed out of frustration and rolled her eyes at the phone screen. Michael hadn't returned her calls or text messages. They would have talked over the phone by now and made plans to go out, specially it being a Saturday. Her first two unanswered text messages and four unreturned phone calls really had her in a fume. After the fourth text and tenth unanswered phone call, she grew worried. She nervously sat on the sofa with phone in hand, occasionally glancing down at it every other second. Have I missed his call, she thought? It's happened before, where the phone doesn't ring, but a call goes straight to voicemail and the voicemail notification pops up on her screen. She scrolled through the call log to reassure herself that it wasn't the case. She stared at the bright screen in disappointment. No missed calls from Michael. She then swiped to the message inbox to check for any new text messages that might have come through but there weren't any. The last message from Michael was the goodnight text he sent last night. Disappointment had settled on her face. She opened Instagram to view his profile and hoped there were something posted to his story; that would at least let her know that he was okay. And if there were something posted, there was going to be hell to pay for not returning her calls. *I swear to God, he better be somewhere like in a village saving children from a barn fire, or have a really damn good excuse for not sending at least a simple hello text.* But there was nothing posted to his story. She scrolled through the feed to pass the time, double tapping on a picture her friend posted. A strong urge to give him another call came over her. She pondered her next decision. Give him another call or send an infuriating text? She got up from the sofa and walked to kitchen as she placed the call. The phone rang loudly on the speaker and repeatedly. She paced from the sofa back to the kitchen as the call kept ringing until it went to voicemail. Call me!" she furiously shouted and tossed the phone to the sofa. From underneath the cupboard, she pulled out a large pan and set in the sink. She opened the faucet and filled it up with water. She then added salt and olive oil. She turned on the stove and place the pan on top to boil the water. She then opened a package of angel hair pasta and tossed the pasta in the pan.

Michael punched through a yellow stop light at fifty miles an hour as he tightly gripped the steering wheel to his black Chevy Camaro like a NASCAR driver on his final lap. He raced through the streets determined to get to the antique store as quickly as possible. He swerved in and out of lanes, never bothering with the blinker. The black leather belt which rested on red passenger seat, wiggled from side to side with every sharp turn. Once a lane opened, he quickly took the opportunity to advance maneuvering through any small gap. A woman in sunglasses driving a gray minivan loudly honked her horn as Michael thoughtlessly cut her off. She pulled up behind him almost tailgating Michael as they both picked up speed. The woman had an enraged look on her face. She shouted obscenities, using every cuss word in the book and flipped the middle finger at him. Michael saw her through the rear-view mirror and for a second thought of slamming on the breaks so that she could crash into him and bust her head open on the steering wheel. He coldly stared at the angered woman who followed him closely. The traffic light turned red and Michael buried his foot into the aluminum gas pedal. The exhaust let out a booming roar as the gleaming Camaro sped through the intersection. Vibrant sun rays bounced off the wide body of the vehicle as it raced toward its destination.

The Camaro's black alloy wheels slowly came to a stop as it pulled in front of the antique store. Michael pushed the shifter into park. A look of disbelief crawled over his face as he stared wide eyed out through tinted passenger window. The rumble of the motor cut as he turned the keys to the ignition. He flung the door open and stepped out, gently closing the door as he kept his eyes fixed on the store. He looked up at the cross streets to reassure himself of the location then walked over to the store. The antique store had boarded-up windows and a corroded security gate with a solid steel padlock. The place looked as if it had been abandoned for years. The plywood was old and faded. The folding security gate was rusty and the padlock lost its shine. He yanked down on the lock trying to open it but it was secured on tight. He clung to the gate in dismay. Next to the abandoned store was a mini market with a neon open sign over the window. Michael decided to go in and ask about the antique store and the whereabouts of its owner.

The door chimed as Michael walked into the fully stocked market. He walked past the chips and up to the counter. There was a dark middle eastern man sitting behind the counter reading the newspaper. Michael cleared his throat to get the man's attention. "Excuse me," Michael said politely staring down at the man, his eyes hidden by the newspaper held up to his face. The man lowered the newspaper just below his nose, peeking over it with an annoyed look. He huffed as if bothered by Michael's presence and his willingness to disturb the man's peace. "Yes, how can I help you?" the man with horseshoe hairline asked. "What happened to the antique shop next door?" asked Michael.

"What antique shop?" asked the man with a puzzled expression.

"The antique shop next door that's now boarded up and locked."

"I have no idea."

"Did you know the owner? An old man with frizzy white hair."

"No. I never met the owner or seen him."

"Well surely you must have seen him before."

"Sir, are you going to buy something?"

Michael reached down the counter and picked up a pack of gum and set it down on the counter with a loud thud. The man reached for the gum and scanned it. "One fifty," he firmly said. Michael pulled out his wallet and handed the man two dollars. The man opened the register and took out two quarters that he set down on the counter. "That place has been shut down for over eight years. As long as I have owned this store, I've never seen it open."

The man's response felt unsettling and left Michael with a baffled expression as he picked up the gum and loose change from the counter to put in his pocket. "But I was just there yesterday. I was inside the antique store. It had old furniture, clothes and a bunch of other stuff, uhm antiques and what not. I was speaking directly with the old man, face to face as I am with you now."

"Impossible," said the man while shaking his head. "You are mistaken my friend. As I already told you, that place has been closed for many years now. There is no antique store there. Are you sure you are on the correct street?"

"I'm positive. Are you certain that you've never seen an old man with creepy black eyes go into that store next door?"

"The only thing creepy is you my friend. I said that it's been closed for a long time now and still you ask me this? Why? I look dumb to you maybe? Huh?"

Michael's fist clenched as he stood before the agitated man ready to knock him out with a square punch to the chin. He envisioned throwing a punch then forcefully slamming the man's head down hard on the counter, busting his nose and breaking his teeth. He saw blood smeared over the counter as it gushed out from the man's nose and trickled out of his toothless mouth. At that moment a young girl walked in and headed toward the rack with chips. Michael unclenched his fists and walked out of the store. The owner kept a serious look as he watched Michael turn and walk out.

Michael stopped in front of the boarded-up store and stared at it with anger. He rattled the security gate with both hands, ferociously tugging at it. As his aggression subsided, he took a step back feeling lost in confusion and leaned up against his car. He stood there gazing at the store as if waiting for it to somehow magically open or hoping to see the old man sluggishly turn the corner. Neither would happen and he knew it, but the mystery of the antique store could not go unsolved and the one person that could save his sanity and reaffirm everything about the store had been blowing up his phone all day. Michael quickly hopped in his car and started the motor. He slammed his foot on the gas pedal while turning the wheel counter clock wise to make a U-turn cutting off oncoming traffic. Motorist honked their horns as Michael sped down the street. The exhaust pipes made a roaring echo as Michael raced to Lilith's place.

Lilith sat at her small kitchen table swirling freshly made pasta with her fork when loud banging at her door made her jolt. She gasped out of fright at the first pound. The fork clinked as it slipped from her fingers and dropped to the plate. "Lilith," Michael screamed from the other side of the door. She jumped out of her chair at hearing his distressed voice and immediately unlocked the door to let him in. "Where have you been?" she demanded standing in front of the door. He rushed inside and stood by the table facing her with a look that concerned Lilith for his wellbeing. "I'll explain everything in just a minute, but for now I need you to please tell me, do you remember the antique store from yesterday with the creepy old dude and the black belt?" he asked wide eyed eager to receive her confirmation. "Yeah, why?" she replied with a perplexed look. Relief quickly spread over his face at hearing her response and he felt at ease. He pulled out a chair and took a seat.

"What's this all about Michael?" her voice filled with concern as she sat back down and slid her plate to the side. Michael picked up the plate and stuffed his mouth with pasta. She was astonished to see how quickly he devoured her meal. "I haven't eaten much all day," he murmured with a mouthful and slurped the pasta noodle in. "I'm starving. Sorry were you going to finish this?"

"There's more," she replied. "Well, what have you been doing all day that you haven't eaten or even bothered to return any of my calls?"

Had it not been for manners at the dinner table, Michael would have licked the plate, but he set the empty plate aside and told Lilith all about his day. He shared the day's events up into the unpleasant conversation he had with the store clerk from the mini market, next to the boarded-up store.

"And that's when I raced over here to ask you about the store. To make sure I'm not going crazy. That what you and I both saw is real. The store, the belt, the old man, all real."

Lilith was flabbergasted and wondered if all he said was true. "But we were there just yesterday," she argued.

"Yes, I know that," he said gesturing at himself with both hands, but the guy at the market said it's been closed for several years now. Oddly enough though, I have to say, by the looks of it, with the boards and rusty gate, it seems like the guy may have been telling the truth."

"This is crazy," she said and shook her head. "I vividly remember walking out and passing up the market, so I know which market you're talking about. It was right next door. I think this guy was messing with you. There's no way the antique store has been closed for several years now. Impossible, we were just there yesterday."

"That's what I kept telling him. But maybe you're right, maybe he was just fucking with me. He looked like a douchebag anyway. And I don't know, maybe the old man couldn't pay the bills and was forced to shut it all down."

"Yes, it's possible. Maybe he fell behind with the rent and business wasn't doing too well. I mean you saw that place, it was full of dust and no one but us were inside. We didn't even buy anything. Only reason we walked out of there with anything was because he gave it to us for free."

He looked at her with uneasy eyes. "Why did you go there anyway?" she asked whilst on the topic. "You said you went back to ask him about the belt and of how he knew all the things you said as a kid."

"Doesn't matter anymore," he somberly said. "I'm just glad I'm not losing my mind. We can both agree that the antique store is real."

"You're not crazy babe. It's real as you and I are." She placed her hand over his and smiled warmly. "Well look, we have Darren's party tonight and hopefully that'll brighten your mood. So, let's plan on what we're going to take to the party and what time we should leave."

Michael went back home to get ready for the party. The shower curtain rings scraped against the rod as Michael slid the curtain and grabbed a towel off the rack. He patted himself dry and stepped in front of the mirror. Steam waltzed around the ceiling dome light fixture. The mirror was clouded, and walls were moist. He tossed the towel around his shoulder and put on his briefs, then wiped the mirror with his hand. It left streaks on the glass while the rest remained wet and cloudy. A loud bang startled him. Sounded like it came from the plumbing. The house was a few years old, built in the 1950's but the plumbing never made a sound like that. Dad's not going to like that. Another costly repair. The mirror then vibrated and his reflection bounced as it shook. Again, the loud bang. He then felt a rumble under his feet and the house cracked as it violently swayed from side to side. He tightly held on to the corners of the sink as he rode the waves of an earthquake. The light above flickered as the bathroom juddered causing sporadic moments of total darkness. In between the flashing of lights, through the murky mirror he saw a towering presence standing behind him with a grimace of rage. Seconds later the shaking stopped and the lights came back on. Michael quickly turned around but found no one. He looked at the cloudy mirror again and wiped it with his towel. His image was the only one staring back in the reflection. He unlocked the bathroom door and swiftly stepped out with his eyes fixed on the mirror. "Hey Elisa," he called out to his sister. "You okay?"

"What?" she yelled in the distance. He walked to her bedroom door and asked again, "are you okay?"

"Yeah, why?" she asked opening the door.

"The earthquake."

"What earthquake?" she asked staring at him with confusion.

"The earthquake just now. Don't tell me you didn't feel it."

"There was an earthquake? Oh my God, I didn't feel anything."

"Yeah, it was pretty big. You had to have felt it, unless you were working out."

"No, I was sitting on my bed looking through my phone. I didn't feel a thing. Are you sure it was an earthquake?"

"Yes. And it lasted for like at least fifteen seconds or more. The whole house shook. The shower curtains swayed, there was loud banging coming from the pipes and the lights turned on and off."

She stood silent for a moment waiting for the punch line thinking it was another one of his jokes, then noticed that his face didn't break and he was dead serious. "That's so weird. I didn't feel or hear anything."

"You sure?"

"I swear."

His eyes looked troubled and walked away feeling baffled.

"Are you okay?" she asked watching him walk back.

He paused and momentarily looked up. The words fought to escape his lips, but his mouth stayed shut. He nodded his head then walked to his room.

He closed the door behind him and grabbed a pair of dark washed jeans from the hanger. His right leg went in followed by the left, then he stopped in the middle of buttoning up. He looked up with an uneasy look. There was a presence in the room watching him dress. He couldn't see it but knew that there was something or someone there coldly staring at him like the ghostly black eyes that he saw in the bathroom mirror. It's the same feeling he had the night before, and the same feeling he's continued to have ever since stepping inside the antique store. It had occurred to him that he might be slowly losing his mind. After all, mental illness was common in his family. Several years ago, an aunt, his mother's sister, would randomly shout at her boyfriend, calling him every name in the book other than what was printed on his government I.D. She'd say nasty things and then act as of nothing ever happened. On one such occasion, they were in her living room watching a sitcom. She lied on the sofa with her head rested on his lap. In the middle of their laughter, she stopped then turned to look up at him and glared with hate. She shouted at him, "get out of my head," and proceeded to scratch his face, cutting his cheek and neck with her long nails. He had to physically restrain her and pin her down on the floor. A minute later, with small drops of blood on her chest that had dripped off her boyfriend's face, she asked him if he was hungry. For days she would go without a meal and suffered from insomnia. It wasn't until one night that he woke up to the sounds of scratching on a wall at three a.m. and found her fully nude facing the corner of the room clawing at the walls and talking to herself. Through the muffled gibberish he could make out what she was saying, "he's returned." He admitted her to the hospital soon after. Michael also had an uncle, Barry, who'd gone around the bend after his wife left him for another man. Cheap whiskey and Malboro Red cigarettes consoled his lonely nights, but also aided in his spiraling health and mental stability. A month later, he lost his job working at an insurance company as a claim's agent. He would show up to work almost an hour late, reeking of alcohol, still drunk from the night before. He'd have full on conversations with himself at his desk. Co-workers thought he was on the phone talking to a client through his headset until one day, Josh, who sat across from Barry decided to unplug the cord from the phone and confirm their suspicions. When they passed Barry's desk, Barry was fully engaged in a conversation with no one on the line. HR terminated him later that day. He was later evicted from his apartment and moved back in with his parents. That lasted a short while. They kicked him out for stealing his mother's jewelry and electric appliances and selling them for booze money. Months later police came knocking on their door asking them to go down to the coroner's office and identify their son's body. He had committed suicide. He used a broken bottle to cut his veins. His body was found next to a dumpster in an alley behind a liquor store.

It was a quarter past ten when Michael and Lilith arrived at the party. Michael had a bottle of whiskey in one hand and held Lilith's hand with the other. A group of young men stood on the porch drinking beer and having a laugh. Their humorous exchange was drowned out by the loud music coming from inside the small house. The front wooden door was wide open, and the party looked to be getting off to a great start. Loud conversations could be heard over pop music that was playing on the soundbar. The music grew louder as Michael and Lilith approached the house. The group of guys on the porch cut their conversation when one of them nodded his head in her direction, shifting their attention on Lilith's bewitching beauty. She wore long black boots with a black skirt that matched her wide brim hat. She walked like models do on a runway, a walk which gave the impression of extreme confidence. She didn't have to stare back at them to know that they were looking, but she gave them a quick glance and a barely noticeable smirk. Michael had grown used to the attention she received. It didn't bother him anymore. In fact, he took it as compliment to know that the girl other men de-sired would be going home with him at the end of the night. He held his head up high and chest out as they walked past the group of ogling boys. She walked in with a cheerful smile observing all the festive and half-drunk partygoers. There was a diverse group of people inside the long and narrow living room all holding a red cup with a concoction of alcohol. Some of them occupied the middle of the living room used for a dance floor while others were seated on the couch drinking and talk-ing loudly. Michael stepped in observing everyone's behavior. He no-ticed a group of girls closely dancing with one another, wooing as they sensually caressed each other's warm bodies while dancing to the mu-sic playing from two loud speakers. Marijuana smoke flowed through the air forming a cloud above the room. A young guy wearing a black hoodie over his head relaxed on the sofa and deeply puffed on a joint and then passed it to one of his buddies seated next to him who watched the girls dance and thrust their hips back and forth. Lilith pulled on Michael's hand leading him through the estrogen and testosterone filled crowd, squeezing by everyone to get to the kitchen. Michael weaved by the group of girls accidentally bumping into one of them causing her to spill her drink onto one of the boys standing on the dance floor. His face changed from a wide-eyed surprised look to disbelief when he looked down at the large stain of alcohol that smelled of cheap vodka spilled over his brand-new tee shirt purchased earlier that day for that particular party, to infuriated eyes that could burn right through her empty red cup. She let out a nervous giggle and pointed at Michael behind her. Lilith easily spotted her friend Darren who stood a few inches taller than the rest as he poured himself a drink. His face lit up as she walked toward him with open arms to give him a hug. Michael followed Lilith and stepped out from the cluster of people when he felt a hand strongly grab him by the shoulder. He was yanked hard and spun around. To his surprise, the blue shirt guy got in his face with flared nostrils, a red face and a hostile look in his eye. Before he could utter a word Michael drove his forehead into the guys face breaking his nose. Blood gushed out of his nostrils pouring onto his shirt. His first reaction was of disbelief at the sight of blood pouring out his nose like an open faucet. His eyes turned watery and then a look of pain covered his face as he felt his twisted nose. A circle formed around the two and Lilith stood close watching the drama unfold with a shocked look on her face. The blue shirt guy's stoner friends pushed their way through the crowd to come to his aid and confronted Michael. Darren, Lilith's tall friend, quickly jumped in between to break it up. Darren's other buddies stepped in to help and kicked out the blue shirt guy and his friends. They pulled on his arms and shoved him out the door yelling at him to get out. If it weren't for Lilith, Darren would have thrown Michael out too.

"What happened?" asked Darren in a curt manner.

"He put his hands on me," Michael replied with a serious look in his eye. Lilith nodded at Darren, letting him know she would look after him and took Michael into the kitchen. She fixed him a drink and then poured herself one too as Michael leaned against the counter.

"Here," she said and handed him a cup filled with juice mixed with vodka. "What happened? Why'd you hit him?"

Michael brought the drink up to his lips and his eyes shifted down in thought. He took a large gulp and made a sour face as the vodka burned down his throat. "He shouldn't have grabbed me like that. You don't grab a man like that and not expect to get hit in the face."

"But it's not like you to just hit a guy, Michael. I saw you. He didn't even get a chance to get a word out before you cracked him with your head breaking his nose." Michael took another drink.

"I don't know. I felt disrespected so I did what I had to get some respect."

She examined his head for swelling. "Does it hurt?" she asked gently placing her fingers on his forehead.

"No, I'm fine," he replied holding her by the waist. She stared into his eyes. "You're crazy," she said with a smile and kissed him on the forehead. He picked up her drink and handed it to her. They cheered and drank from the cup. As the night carried on, Michael poured themselves another drink. His fifth and her third. He carried the drinks to the dance floor, spilling some it along the way. She took it from his hand and cheered him before taking a sip. She turned around and backed herself into him. He grabbed her by the waist and held her close. Her hair brushed against his face as he dug his face into her neck, kissing and licking her neck and shoulder. They sensually danced moving side to side, his pelvis rubbing against her butt. She rang her fingers through his hair. Her eyes kept shut, feeling the ecstasy of the moment and his erection rub against her back. He turned her around and firmly grabbed her ass. Their tongues swirled in and around each other's mouth.

"Let's go home," she whispered into his ear with lust in her eyes. She grabbed his hand and walked out the door.

"I had so much fun," she slurred.

"Yeah, I had fun too," he said holding her hand as they walked to the car parked down the block by a stop sign.

She leaned against the car trying to keep her balance as he opened the door. She held onto his arm and clumped in the seat. She folded down the visor and looked in the mirror to fix her hair. Michael turned the keys to the ignition and she turned the volume knob to max and loudly played the radio. She snapped her fingers with her eyes half shut and waved her arms in a dance while Michael steered the wheel with his left and felt on her inner thigh with his right. He stared at her with salacious eyes as she guided his hand up closer to her vagina. He caressed her soft skin before sliding his finger under her panties. She bit her lips and tilted her back as he felt her warmth and moist. She let out a soft moan as she spread her legs further apart. His fingers dug deep inside her and her breathing was heavier and moans were louder. Suddenly they felt a bump in the road which made them jolt in their seat and Michael slammed on the breaks and cut the radio.

"What was that?" she asked.

"I think I hit something," Michael replied with a worried look.

"Something? Or someone?" she nervously asked.

He opened the car door and stepped out. They were in the middle of the street in a quiet neighborhood. A few porch lights were on but all of the lights in every house were off. The rumble of the engine was the only sound. Michael stepped behind the car to take a look and didn't see anything. He crouched and looked under the car and didn't see anything either. He then heard a hissing sound. His ear was next to the exhaust pipe so he couldn't quite make out what it was. He stood up and stood still waiting to hear a sound. As he stood motionless, his eyes looked around and then he heard the hissing again followed by a long low-pitched moan. He followed the cries to a couple of yards away from his car and as he got closer to the sidewalk, there he a found a badly wounded cat laying on its side by a tree. Its hind legs were broken. The moribund cat hissed, barely able to lift its head. Michael crouched down to pet it. He looked back to the car and saw Lilith waiting in the car.

"Oh, you poor thing," he softly said, gently patting its back. His hand glided from the cat's crushed stomach up to its neck, feeling the softness of its black fur, its warmth and tremble underneath his palm. His thumb came under the cat's throat while his long fingers stretched out firmly wrapping around the cat's brittle neck and squeezed with might. The cat fiercely hissed as Michael wrapped both hands around its neck. Michael's nostrils flared and his lips raised like a snarling dog as he chocked the life out of the cat. Within seconds the cat was motionless and a look of gratification came over Michael's face as he released his strong grip on the lifeless animal. He stood watching over it in a callous manner then looked back to his car to check on Lilith. Her silhouette still in the passenger seat. He looked down at the dead cat with its tongue out and eyes open. It was the first time he'd ever seen anything dead in real life. It was also the first time he'd ever taken a life. He turned and hurried back to his car.

"What happened?" Lilith asked with concern.

"Oh, nothing. I was taking a piss behind the tree."

"What was that bump we felt?"

"It was a just big rock laying in the middle of the street. I picked it up and left it by the tree," he said putting the gear shifter into drive and speeding off.

Lilith raised a skeptic eye brow, "oh, okay." She relaxed her head against the leather headrest and slouched in the seat. Her head slid down as her heavy eyes surrendered to sleep. During the drive to her apartment, Michael replayed the scene in his head over and again. His fingers gripping the cat's neck. The animal's struggle. It's front paws dangling as it took its last breath. I put it out of its misery. It was suffering. I did the right thing. It was late. No one was around to help and it's not my cat so I can't get stuck with paying for its medical expenses. No, I did the right thing by ending its life and putting it out of its misery. But why did you take pleasure in killing it? I didn't. I ... I ... I've had too much to drink tonight. People do things they normally wouldn't do when sober. It was ... it was ... it was exciting. No, I mean, necessary. No, it was godawful and unnecessary. But I ended its misery. I did good by it. It's not suffering anymore.

Michael battled with his own thoughts during the drive, reflecting on his appalling actions and justifying them as an act of kindness toward an already dying animal. Cruelty would have been to let it suffer any longer than need be. He parked in front of Lilith's apartment and stared at her. She was in deep sleep with her head rested against the window. Hair covered her face. He knew there was no sense in trying to wake her. She'd pass out like this before on numerous occasions after a night of heavy drinking. Like many times before, he'd have to grab her purse, throw her arm around his neck, lift her out of the car, kick the door closed and carry her up to the apartment. This night proved to be the same. He stepped out of the car and went around to her door and opened it. He crouched to grab her purse lying by her feet when he noticed a rolled up black leather belt underneath the seat. Images of the cats lifeless eyes and tongue flashed through his head. A shudder ran through him as he picked up the belt. Not possible. What's it doing here? It was supposed to be in his room underneath the bed just as he had left it. His mind quickly raced for an explanation. Did I bring it with me? Did I forget? Lilith moaned turning in her seat, still asleep. Michael set the belt back down and grabbed her purse. He positioned her arm around his neck, placed his arm underneath her thighs and lifted her up.

Once inside, he gently placed her down on the bed with her head rested on a pillow. He unzipped her boots and pulled them off her feet, carefully setting them down on the floor beside the bed. He pulled the cover over her and turned off the bedside lamp then sat on the edge of the bed reflecting in the dark. He stared out the window looking up at the silvery glow of the moon as his mind wandered back to the street of where he committed his monstrous act. The cats front paws dangling as he squeezed the animals throat replayed in his mind. He lowered his head and buried his face in his hands then immediately popped his head out and looked down at them with a sickened expression. He rushed toward the bathroom and turned the faucet on. The cold water swished and formed air bubbles as it ran. He furiously scrubbed his hands together with soap. Foam and bubbles coated his hands as he frantically rubbed them together nearly peeling his skin, then rinsed them underneath the running water. He rubbed his hands thoroughly for a few minutes, staring at himself in the mirror above the sink when he noticed a shadowy figure move across the room behind him. He turned around and saw Lilith standing in the doorway, fully nude. She stared at him with lust. He stared back like a hungry wolf looking to devour. Her tiny bare feet softly padded on the white tile floor as she approached. She took his hand and looked at him with entrancing eyes then put his middle finger in her mouth and sucked. He stared at her mouth as she worked the finger then felt on her pointy full breasts, caressing and hardening the nipples with his thumb. He put his arm around her small waist to pull her in close and lifted her up, holding her by her butt. She wrapped her long and toned legs around him and hung onto his neck, kissing and biting his bottom lip. He carried her to the bed and laid her down with him on top. As their tongues danced with one another, she used both hands to unbutton his jeans and undo his zipper. Her hand slid through and made her way under his briefs. She tugged. Their hearts raced with each passionate kiss. He pulled down his pants and used the front of his boot to hold down the heel of his other boot to slip out of it. She felt the firmness in her palm and guided it to her entry. He licked the tip and slowly slid into her. Her head tilted back and her eyes rolled up as she let out a soft loud moan. Pleasurable sighs resonated through the dark bedroom with every stroke. Street light and the milky radiance of the moon shined through the window. Her nails clawed at his muscular back. His hips thrusted back and forth diving deep into her rapturing realm. Their warm bare bodies would continue to entwine with each other throughout the night until reaching the peak of pleasure.

Chapter 4

Elisa danced in front of the bathroom mirror as she brushed her teeth. The song Raspberry Beret by Prince played on her phone. She had various playlists with almost every genre. From hip-hop to rock-n-roll. The song of her selection would most definitely depend on her mood. If the sun was bright and her mood matched its radiance, then the song was a jovial one. She stepped to the right shaking her tight hips then swung them to the left, holding the toothbrush like a microphone and jubilantly sang the chorus. She hummed the lyrics as she brushed in a circular motion. Brown hair strands fell over her round face as she danced around the sink in a white cropped tee shirt and purple panties. Every morning she would start the day by dancing in the mirror. It helped with putting herself in a good mood and creating a positive mindset. The movement also got her blood flowing and target muscles that have been stiff for several hours. She gargled and rinsed then smiled brightly in the mirror. Her pearly white teeth looked a lot better than last week before going in to her dentist's office for a teeth whitening procedure. That day she took over twenty selfies and posted the best one to her Instagram without a filter to show off her radiant smile. That morning, as routine, she'd wear a sports crop top and leggings with a pair of comfortable grey and white running shoes to hit the gym, but first she would make a healthy breakfast.

Elisa cracked another egg on the counter and gently dropped it in the hot pan. The eggs sizzled as it spread out on the pan. She grabbed an empty water bottle from the counter and placed the opened top over the yolk and squeezed the bottle, sucking the yolk into the bottle. It was a trick she learned on YouTube of how to easily remove yolk from the pan. She tossed the high in cholesterol and fatty egg yolks to the trash as the pan hissed. While the egg whites cooked over medium heat, she cut an avocado in half. Toast popped up and the bread was warm and golden brown. She spread avocado over both slices of bread then placed the egg whites over each slice and made herself a cup of coffee using the Keurig machine next to the toaster. She sat at the table and read a self-help book for women titled *Girl, Please* in bold red letters. The toast crunched as she bit it. Crumbs fell to her plate. She flipped the page and continued to read on about the importance of realizing how amazing she already is and to start acting like it which'll lead to her becoming an unstoppable force, a fearless woman, one without limits. Another bite to fuel her body and a few more pages to feed her mind. After a few minutes, she put the dish in the sink and ran upstairs to grab her keys and purse. As routine, right after breakfast, she'd head straight to her local gym just four miles south from her home.

She walked in the two-story gym with high energy and motivation, ready to break a sweat and put herself in some serious pain. The girl at the counter next to the turnstile gate looked up from her phone and smiled at Elisa who scanned her pass. As Elisa walked through and made her way down the stairs she heard the familiar sounds that envelops a gym. Pop music on the ceiling speakers, heavy breathes and loud exhales, the thudding of weights and dumbbells down on the black rubber mat and metal clinking. The lower level was a bit smaller than upstairs by a few feet, but the long and wide mirrors that covered the walls gave it a much larger appearance. At the turn she saw the regular gym rats working up a sweat and grunting, except for two new faces who broke concentration at seeing her walk toward the inner/outer thigh machine. A bald guy with protruding veins on his temple and red face, curled a fifty-pound dumbbell. Droplets of saliva flew out of his mouth as he huffed and grunted bringing the heavy dumbbell up toward his face.

Bulging veins ran down his massive biceps to his wide forearms. He would be described as a nurse's dream the way his veins popped out. Today was arm day. He focused on working on all three muscles of the bicep by doing preacher curls, dumbbell hammer curls, standing barbell curls and cable curls. At a glance, no one would be able to guess that at one point in his life, he was seventy pounds overweight, an alcoholic, and suffered from severe depression. Obesity was something he had struggled with all his life. Early in his childhood, kids at school would tease him, often calling him names like miss piggy and never picked him to be part of a team whenever the kids played a game like basketball or soccer. Later as an adult, married and still overweight, he would fall into depression after discovering that his wife of five years was having an affair with a co-worker. That would explain all the long hours at work or the numerous "happy hour" get togethers with co-workers. Alcohol followed thereafter and the answers to all his problems could never be found at the bottom of that bottle of liquor, no matter how desperately he searched, nonetheless he would go on a quest for them every single night. It wasn't until one day, he got out of bed, groggy, feeling tired of being depressed and alone with a breath that reeked of whiskey, that he decided enough was enough. He grabbed the half empty bottle from the nightstand and poured it out in the bathroom sink. The bottle glugged as he stared at the mirror. In the reflection, with tears forming in his eyes, he saw the strength and determination of man that would carry him through a long and weary battle. Self-help books replaced the bottle on the nightstand and kept him company on several lonely nights. A gym membership kept his mind distracted and away from the painful memories of a time he longed for. The gym, books, and healthy meal prepping kept him busy with trying to become a better version of himself every day. Years later, he would remarry, live a happy and sober life and continue to work out at the gym without missing a day and today was arm day.

A bulkier guy, not as toned, but with wide arms and tree trunks for legs, stood by the long barbell, psyching himself up for a deadlift with heavy metal blasting through his earphones. He stepped up to the bar getting into position, bending his knee to lift and placed his heavy hands over the metal bar, keeping them close to his shins. He took in three deep breaths, lifted his chest, looked up and pulled the 350-pound bar as he stood up straight with his chest out and shoulders rolled back. He let out a loud grunt as he came up with the bar, eyes wide and intense, nose flaring as he stood tall holding the metal bar. He exhaled through his mouth and then dropped it. Others occupying different machines targeting different areas of the body carried on with their workout as did Elisa who sat on a leg machine working her thighs. She squeezed and brought her thighs together, feeling each repetition get harder than the last. The muscles in her inner thighs felt tight. She winced, squeezing with all her might. The weight stack on the machine raised up as her knees came together. After finishing her set, she got up, legs slightly trembling and pulled the pin out of the weight stack, placed it over another rectangular plate decreasing the weight, flipped the cushions keeping them outside of her knees and repeated the motion, only this time pushing her thighs out. For the next hour she used different machines targeting her legs and glutes.

Inside the locker room with wide mirror beside the entrance next to the sinks, she took a selfie pointing the camera at the mirror with her hips pushed out and hand on the waist. She struck different poses, taking a picture in several angles, using the ceiling lights to create the perfect snapshot. Using the twelfth shot, she posted the photo to her Instagram story.

A mile away from the gym was a restaurant that specialized in salads and wraps. It had an outdoor seating area adorned with plants where she would frequent after working out. She stood in line waiting to place an order, browsing Instagram stories. Two tall firefighters in front of her with wide shoulders ordered the 'mighty wrap', one of the restaurants signature wraps that came with BBQ chicken, corn and all the greens. Their walkies hung by the side clipped to their yellow fire pants.

Elisa momentarily glanced up to stare at both men that towered over her then quickly reverted her eyes to the screen scrolling through Instagram and laughing at memes. She viewed her brother's story. He uploaded a video of himself at a scenic park that stretched around several hills overlooking much of the city.

A bright yellow sun hung over the clear midday sky. Fluffy white clouds formed sundry shapes over the city's large skyscrapers. Atop of a dirt hill with picturesque hiking trails, Michael sat in the shade of a tree overseeing the cities bustle and people watching. From afar, cars seemed like small toys, like the one's he used to play with as a child. Often, he'd pretend to race two cars side by side, pushing them along with his little fingers making sounds of engines revving. Then one would lose control and crash into the other causing it to flip and roll. He'd make an explosion sound and imitate the agonizing screams of someone burning inside the wreck. The people below appeared to be the size of ants carrying on with their busy day. A white and blue helicopters rotor blades chopped through the air as it flew above the neighborhood surrounding downtown. Michael sat, lost in thought. His droopy and dark circled eyes fashioned by a sleepless night, stared off in the distance.

The night before, as Lilith lied asleep with her head rested on Michael's chest, Michael stared up at the celling wide awake like an insomniac unable to sleep. The milky white moon moved across the dark sky over the course of the night. The hours elapsed and Michael's head overflowed with thoughts that swam around his brain. The creepy old man from the antique store came to mind along with the haunting tale of the werewolf of Bedburg and all the things he read online. He thought of the brutal incident with the cat and the satisfaction he got out of taking its life made him question everything he knew about himself. The act itself presented him with a question, what else was he capable of? Hours seemed like minutes as they hurried through the night. Just before five a.m. he forced his eyes closed at an attempt to fall asleep. The sound of Lilith's heavy breathing and gentle snores were the only sounds from inside the bedroom until an abrupt faint yowling forced his eyes open. Michaels wide eyes looked around the dark room inspecting each corner, listening attentively. From underneath the bed, a long-drawn-out yowl commanded his attention. He quickly turned to his side to look down at the floor. Impossible he thought. She doesn't own a cat, in fact she's allergic. Hissing sounds followed and Michael swiftly leapt out of bed with curiosity. He kneeled beside the bedframe in search of the creature. Underneath the bed he beheld a pair of bright yellow eyes with a thin black slit that glowed. Its shape was unclear with the absence of light, but its fierce hissing made it evident that it was a cat. Michael was dumbfounded and sat on the floor gazing at the cats spellbinding eyes.

"What's wrong?" Lilith asked with a sleepy face looking down at Michael.

"The cat," Michael answered apprehensively pointing underneath the bed frame.

"What cat?" she asked with eyes half shut.

"The one underneath your bed."

"There's no cat under the bed."

"Yes, there is, I just saw it."

"Look again."

Michael cautiously inched forward fearing a slash to the face from the feral cat lurking below. He peeked underneath once again but found it empty. The cat was gone. Perhaps it crept out in stealth. Then a low creak came from the floorboard where the cat was seen. Michael tilted his head with his ear to the floor. Just as he lowered his head a loud bang came from below that made him jolt followed by scraping against the wood. The clawing sounds continued for a brief moment followed by another bang, louder and fierce. The panels slit before cracking open and out of the floor sprung out a ferocious hairy beast with eyes that sparkled like the moon. It's long sharp fangs the size of an average man's finger covered in drool, dripped from its long snout. Its pointed black claws lunged forward causing Michael to topple over. The beast climbed on top of Michael and dug deep into his chest with its knife-like claws piercing through the flesh and tearing deep into the muscle. Michael yelled in agony as blood dripped from his open wound. The beast snarled intensely puffing hot air through its wet black snout, looking down at its prey pinned to the ground with its claws drilled deep into the wet and warm flesh, staring at itself through the reflection of Michaels agonizing eyes. Its jaws opened wide. Drops of thick saliva dripped from its long and rough tongue onto Michael's face. Its warm breath smelled of dry blood and its long white fangs came straight down and clamped onto Michaels face, tearing through his cheeks and ripping his face. He then felt an aggressive tug on his shoulder and was wakened from the terrifying nightmare.

"Wake up babe," Lilith said half asleep. "You're having another nightmare."

His disoriented eyes scared Lilith and put her in a panic when he tightly grabbed her by the wrist. "Ow! You're hurting me," she cried trying to free herself from his grip. "Michael!" she shouted with fear in her eyes trying to shake free.

"I'm sorry," he said confused as he got up from the bed. His body glistened with sweat. The sheets and pillow damp from where he had laid. He walked to the bathroom sink and splashed water over his face. The cool water dripped down his chin as he stared at himself in the mirror. He wondered what the time could be but thought it close to four or five in the morning. The water running from the faucet splashed creating water bubbles. Lilith turned it off. She stood behind him, wearing an open robe pressing her perky breasts against his back, and softly kissing his shoulder. "Are you okay?" she asked looking at him through the mirror. He stared back with a livelier face. "I'm fine. I'm sorry if I hurt you."

She put her wrist up to his eyes. They had pink ring marks around them.

"I like it rough, but not that rough," she said with a smirk.

He kissed her wrist and apologized again before leading her back to bed. She'd fall asleep by his side again while he remained wide awake watching the colors of the night turn from pitch black to a misty grey then a light blue with the rise of the sun.

Later that morning she went to work, and with the day off from work, he decided to go for a hike to clear his mind. The vibrant sun was high and beating down his neck. The long shadow cast by the baking sun followed closely by his side. A single drop of sweat slid down his neck. His worn out black running sneakers kicked up dirt as he walked zombielike through the park, moving forward on a dirt path with small rocks, and surrounding sage scrub that led up a hill. As he came over the hill, he found an oak tree by the edge offering shade. He sat underneath the tree with his back rested against the bark. A slight breeze came over his face. He closed his eyes and was taken with delight by the wind that cooled his face and dried the sweat off his neck. He looked down at the city in awe of its beauty and decided to share the scenic view on Instagram. He held the phone up taking video of the panoramic scene. After having tramped through the 308-acre recreation area and gone all night without an ounce of sleep, fatigue caught up and overtook his body. His head slumped and he fell into a deep slumber. Minutes later his eyes darted about. He was having another bad dream. Michael found himself at the same park. It was pitch black and the sound of crickets chirping echoed through the night. Small critters dashed through the bushes. The park was poorly lit with old streetlamps that desperately needed maintenance. Several lights that lined up along the pathway were broken. The moon hardly lit the sky making it difficult to see yards away. He followed the same trail he had taken to exit the park and along the way, he heard a jogger quickly approach. The jogger was breathing hard and trotting at a steady pace. The shape of the jogger came closer, and he could make out the outline of a woman. The lights flickered as she sped up. The bulbs flashed rapidly with each step. Just as she advanced to the next light pole, it shut off followed by another keeping the woman's face in the dark. Curious to make out her face, Michael slowed his pace to try and get a look when she passed by. The sound of her feet pushing off the dirt as she ran got louder. She held something at her side that dangled with her movement. At first, he mistook it to be a snake from the outline of its shape and length. It seemed odd for a woman to be running in a lonely park at night with a snake in her hand. Michael took a few steps forward to the next light pole and stood underneath waiting for her to pass. As she got closer, the light bulb above flickered and exploded. He squinched and covered his head to protect him from the falling glass. The glass dropped and shattered by his feet, nearly missing him. He opened his eyes to look up and the woman was gone. He instantly turned around in search of the woman who had vanished in thin air. All he could see was darkness. The glass crunched as he stepped over it while searching for the mysterious woman. Then he felt something underneath his shoe. It wasn't glass, but something stronger that made a clinking sound. He carefully grabbed it and held it up facing the light pole with a working light. It was a belt. There was no way that it was his belt he thought. He ran with it toward the next light pole. He reached the pole and examined it underneath the light. The same metal belt buckle. The same wolf designs. The same black belt the old man had given him. Michaels intense eyes looked in all directions of the park in search of the mysterious woman who dropped the belt down at his feet but there was no one around. Michael's head spun in confusion. The whereabouts of the disappearing woman gave him a fright that propelled his legs forward in a haste to exit the park. The exit was a twenty-minute walk, a distance he would cut in half by sprinting with belt in tow. Down a steep hill he paused in mid stride and stood still; frozen by an unnerving sound just yards away from where he stood. The sound drew nearer, and the sound of rocks pressed against dirt got louder. The sound of footsteps raised his heartbeat with every thud. Fear of the unknown overtook his senses and in a desperate attempt to protect himself from what could be lurking in the dark on this strange night, Michael hurriedly wrapped the belt around his waist. The sound of thundering footstep's got closer and Michael rushed to fasten the belt. He fumbled to place the prong through the notch and the strap slid down to his side. He looked around with panic while trying to get the prong through the hole of the strap. He pulled on the strap and pushed the prong through securing the belt. The next moment he woke up to the sounds of birds chirping outside of his bedroom window. His eyes slowly came into focus and head raised above the pillow. He was in his room laying down on the bed, wearing his normal sleepwear, a tee-shirt and shorts. He looked down at his shirt and shorts feeling perplexed and unable to explain how he made it home. So many questions raised through his head. How did I get here? When did I get home? Why can't I remember? Was it all just a bad dream? He sat on the edge of the bed with his hair disheveled. He looked down at the belt beside his foot, gazing at it strangely then kicked it with his heel underneath the bed. It occurred to him to check his phone. But where was it? His eyes wandered over to the side of the pillow, then scanned the entire room. His car keys where on the nightstand and so was an old receipt from taco bell. He checked under the bed and found it turned off. He powered it back on and found a dozen messages, one vibrating after the other as they came through. All from his girlfriend asking for his whereabouts. After the fourth text, she was getting pretty upset. The message 'WHERE ARE YOU??!!!' written all in caps with question marks and exclamation points were a dead giveaway of how livid she was. By the tenth message, she was seeing red and he was marked for death. Thoughts of an excuse raced through his head because this one, albeit true as it were, was unexplainable and not believable. He could just picture the argument in his head, yeah right, you expect me to believe you somehow lost track of 12 hours between last night and this morning and somehow mysteriously woke up in your bed not knowing how you got there and that your phone was off?! How stupid do you think I am Michael? What do you take me for? An idiot? Not a discussion he was looking forward to. Nevertheless, he sent her a text message letting her know he must have passed out last night and forgot to send her a message.

He went downstairs to the kitchen to grab some water. His sister was sitting at the table having a bowl of oatmeal and going through her phone.

"Morning," Elisa said momentarily looking up at her brother. "Long night I see."

He moaned an unintelligible 'morning' and proceeded for the refrigerator door.

"Hey were you at Kessler Park yesterday? I saw your post."

"I was," he said drinking from a bottle of water.

"Saw on the news today that police found the remains of a girl there this morning."

The water bottle dropped to the floor, spilling cold water around his feet. He stared at her with a blank face. She looked up at him in confusion at hearing the bottles thump. A look of concern washed over his face as water guzzled out of the botte onto the floor. He stood by the counter motionless and in shock. "Are you okay?" she asked.

"Who was she?"

"I don't know."

"Well do they know who did it? What did it say?" he bombarded her with rapid questions.

"I don't know, I didn't read the article. I just read the articles title about a woman's mutilated and half eaten body found this morning at the same park you were at yesterday. It's all over the news and social media."

She held her phone out to him to show him the post about the incident. Michael grabbed her phone and clicked on the articles link. His eyes frantically skimmed through the Los Angeles Times article.

"A man went on his regular morning jog when he noticed something odd sticking out of the shrubs that run along a trail path. As he got closer, he saw a hand sticking out of the shrubs. The hand was covered in dry blood with touches of wet dirt and soil underneath her fingernails. Upon closer inspection, in between the plants he found the half-eaten corpse of a young woman in her early twenties. Her tongue and right eye were missing, as well as facial tissue which appeared to have been torn off with a sharp and pointy object. Her torso was eaten through as if devoured by an animal. The meat on her left leg was gone and only pieces of flesh dangled from the exposed bone down to her shin. She was still wearing her shoe. Detectives would later find her other shoe along with car keys and cell phone closer to the other side of where the trail begins. They believe that is where she was snatched from and then dragged for several yards to where the jogger found her. The jogger who was in a state of shock and vomiting was questioned but not placed under arrest. Although the mutilated body has scratches and bite marks that are consistent with that of a wild animal such as a mountain lion, homicide has not been ruled out and the investigation is ongoing. Police have no leads or eyewitnesses. The park doesn't have cameras and detectives say the only camera facing the entrance to the park is from a house across the recreational area who had a power outage the night before the tragic incident and did not power back on properly. They identified the young woman as Jenny Auster, a senior at Cal State Long Beach who was a few months away from graduating and receiving a bachelor's degree in marketing.

Michael was slumped down on the chair of the kitchen table finishing the article. His eyes couldn't read fast enough as they sped through each sentence.

"Sounds like a Bear did it," commented Elisa scraping the spoon against the bowl.

"There are no Bears at Kessler Park. Are there?"

"Mountain lion then."

"It's possible. Says here the California Department of Fish and Wildlife receive hundreds of mountain lion sighting reports each year. And that half of California is considered mountain lion habitat. Had to be a mountain lion. Had to be."

"It would be terrifying if it wasn't. Can you imagine someone actually doing those things. What type of sick person could bring themselves to do that to that poor girl."

He looked at her with troubling eyes. "Someone not right in their head." He got up from the table and went back up to his room.

He sat on the bed troubled by the incident. He thought of several things. One thing he was relieved about was that there were no clues or evidence of the murderer, assuming the poor girl was indeed murdered. The phone vibrated. It was Lilith. Call me please, I'm worried, read the text. His reply, I'm sorry for not answering. I have a lot to talk to you about but not over the phone. Can I come over?

On the drive to Lilith's apartment, Michael contemplated on telling her the truth. He wondered how crazy it may sound telling her that he may have killed someone but had no recollection of it. She loved him, this he was sure of, but was her love strong enough to keep a secret of this magnitude and would she keep loving him despite what he thinks he might have done.

At the door she greeted him with a cold stare and arms crossed. His head hung low, shyly looking up and quickly withdrew his eyes. If looks could kill, hers hung him by the neck. "Can I come in?" he asked timidly. She stepped aside keeping her piercing eyes on him as he stepped through the door. She closed the door behind her and leaned her back against it. "Are you going to be truthful with me Michael?" He gently took her by the hand and led her to the sofa. "I promise to tell you the truth." He sat facing her placing his hands on her knees. For the next ten minutes, he told her about yesterday evening and of his anomalous morning, but he never told her of the girl in the park, his blackout or of the news about the grisly murder. She argued her stance on the matter, and he placed himself in her shoes. After much back and forth, the two were silent. The only sound was a humming noise coming from the refrigerator. The two didn't have much left to say. All there was to say was already said and for fear of scaring her away, he kept some fear-provoking details to himself. "I swear I don't know what happened. All I know is, I woke up this morning without knowing how I got there. That's the truth. I hope you can believe me." He got up and let himself out.

The next day, Michael started his 9 a.m. shift at Pricemark, a general merchandise retailer. He began with unloading pallets that were brought in early in the morning. The stacked high 7-foot pallets contained new inventory such as pots and electronics like the new electric grill by chef celebrity Vincent Cartellio. He filled the empty shelves with merchandise, carefully placing them in its respective location. His coworker Gisselle who was working the other side of the aisle, in makeup and beauty, glanced and smiled at him. "Morning Gisselle," he said aloud projecting his voice across the aisle. She placed the nail polish on the shelf and walked toward him. "Good morning," she said brushing her hair behind her ear. They both wore a white tee shirt with blue jeans and a green vest with Pricemark's logo printed above the right pocket. "Made it on time today?" she asked. "Just barely, with a minute to spare. "Wow getting better I see."

"Yeah, one warning from Claire is enough for me."

Claire, a middle-aged mother of two was the store supervisor and really liked Michael, but if there was one thing she hated was tardiness. She couldn't fathom how someone could be late for work. If she could get her ass up at the crack of dawn, make breakfast and get the kids ready for school, drop them off, pump gas, sit thru traffic and make it to work thirty minutes before her shift, then everyone else can. She gave Michael a firm warning not to make it a habit.

"You don't want to get on her bad side," Gisselle said watching as Michael placed another box on the bottom shelf. "I heard she can be a total bitch."

"Really? How is she with you?"

"She's cool with me. But I've heard stories."

"Well let's hope I don't become the character in another one of her stories."

"So did you do anything fun over the weekend?"

"Wouldn't really call it fun, but I got into a small fight at a party."

"Oh my god, are you okay? Who's party?"

"Yeah, I'm fine. It all happened so fast. It was my girlfriend's friend's party."

"Oh, you're still with her?"

"Yeah, why?"

"I thought you guys broke up. Last time you said you two had gotten into a fight."

"We did but we didn't break up. We actually got into another huge fight yesterday. We haven't talked since."

"Seems like you guys are always fighting. Need to find yourself a girl that's more understanding."

He smiled up at her catching her drift and played along. "That type of girl is so hard to come by though."

"Oh, they're out there. Some closer than you think."

"Where? Like here? In front of me?" he asked standing close to her.

"Me? Oh no, I love a good fight. The dramatic kind where everyone has to know all of my business because of how loud I am. And I can get loud," she flirted back. "Besides all those fights you two have, makes me think you're just trouble."

"Trouble? Not so much. More like someone who is far from boring."

"Well I got to get back to work or I'll be the one getting chewed out by Claire. But I don't have a ride home. Think you can give me a lift after work? I mean if it's not too much trouble?"

"Of course, I can."

"Great. Don't leave without me," she said walking back to her post with a grin.

The store opened at eight a.m. and customers started trickling in for their everyday needs. The morning crowd, mostly older people, the carpe diem kind that went to bed early at nine thirty p.m. and woke up at seven a.m. would be hours ahead in executing their goals for the day than those who chose to wake up after eight a.m. There were also a few over thirty who stopped in for other things like a new microwave because theirs broke down the day before. Or a box of coffee pods for the office. Each one with their own story to tell walked up and down the aisles pushing a green cart, filling it with everything from medicine to bananas. The cash registers opened to withdraw money, the scanners on the self-checkout beeped, green carts were jarred loose from each other. Workers organized items on a shelf and Michael was in the kitchen department restocking small appliances. The argument with Lilith replayed in his head and the guilt of possibly having something to do with the girl murdered at the park weighed heavy on his mind. A misplaced small box with a toaster inside on the edge of the shelf tipped over and fell just as Claire shuffled by. She stopped in midstride at hearing the clunk and roll of the box. She looked down at it then saw the other boxes placed up on the top shelf and estimated the force of the fall and its possible damage. Michael looked down at the box then up at Claire who was now marching toward him with a furious look and a wide mouth that was salivating at the thought of chewing him up. Michael bent down to pick up the box. "If that thing is broken, are you going to pay for it?" she asked as if she owned ninety percent of stock in the company. He stood silent with a bothered look in his eye holding the box. "No, I didn't think so. Be careful of how you place these things Michael. I don't want to have to tell you again." The fire in her blue eyes was quickly put out by Michael's piercing cold stare. Her frowned eyebrows had arched with fear. She wisely backed off. A little talk back or plain dismissal for being an obnoxious boss would have been ideal rather than having to suffer the torment of his discomforting silence and chilling dark eyes. Her lips moved to speak but she swallowed her words and turned around instead. She turned left at the end of the aisle and kept walking.

Claire walked with a fast pace, looking over her shoulder. As store supervisor for some years, she's had strong words with several of her staff, past and present. Discipling employees was a task she was very accustomed to. Her experience taught her that every person will treat the correction or disciplinary action in their own way. Some have complete meltdowns and turn the water faucet all the way, others throw a tantrum and huff with their chest, while others take it with a grain of salt, and there are the few that learn from it and appreciate the guidance. But all the experience in the world couldn't prepare her for the haunting confrontation she had with Michael. The pupils in his eyes turned a pitch black and there was a deep void in them that made her tremble with fear. Staring into his eyes felt as if she were flapping her arms wildly while falling deep into a black hole that went on forever. She cogitated on what action should be taken or if any. It was a simple mistake, and the box was intact, no indentation or crushed in corners. The warning would suffice. Howbeit, he frightened her.

Claire walked by the grocery department and saw Gisselle placing jars of tomato sauce on the shelf. She looked over her shoulder and approached with timorous steps.

"What's wrong Claire?" Gisselle asked at noticing the distressed look on her face.

"Did you sense anything strange with Michael this morning?" Claire asked in a low voice. She looked around which Gisselle quickly understood that she didn't want anyone else listening in on their conversation. "No, he seemed fine to me," Gisselle replied softly.

She questioned the strength of their relationship and wondered if Gisselle had been truthful or if she would lie for him.

"He's usually a chipper guy. I hope he's not on any kind of drugs. I know plenty a man that's spiraled out of control soon as the girlfriend or wife up and walks out on them. Hurts their pride. So they take to booze or worse the powder. Anything that'll numb the pain of being alone with only the shadows of yesterday to keep them company. Tormenting thing and I sure hope Michaels as bright as he looks, doesn't get caught up in any sort of addiction. Would be a shame to have to fire him for something like that. Not an easy thing to do ya' know? Firing someone because of their addiction. Had to let a young fella go a few years back. He'd come in late and reek of cheap tequila, the kind you'd disinfect a tattoo needle with. Turned out his girlfriend died in a nasty car accident after leaving the bar with 2 of her friends. Slammed head on with a truck. Her scalp was peeled back; legs and arms twisted like a pretzel. Firefighters had to use the jaws of life to get the mangled lifeless bodies of her friends out of the back. The boy took the death of his beloved very hard. Drunk himself to sleep every night. Anyhow, after so many warnings and write ups, I had to let him go. I'd hate to let anyone of my staff go but it's part of the job. So, if you notice anything strange about Michael, please make sure to let me know, will you?"

Gisselle nodded her head in accordance and went back to stacking jars on the shelf. She couldn't wait to tell Michael what Claire had said. Just a few more hours for their shift to end and she'd be alone with Michael in his car.

It was six o'clock and their shift had ended and they both met up at the front. She brushed her dirty blonde hair from her thin face and smiled brightly as Michael exited the front sliding door. He walked in a slow pace, his hands tucked in his bomber jacket pockets and nodded at her.

"Ready to go?" he asked.

"I'm ready," she replied. He led her to his car parked on the side of the store and hit the unlock button on the key fob.

"Thanks again for taking me home. I really appreciate it," Gisselle said opening the door.

"No problem," he replied and got in.

He was quiet. Not saying much, only enough to keep the conversation flowing. His mind was elsewhere. Concentrated on Lilith and the murdered girl from the park. He was present but not mentally and Gisselle could tell his mind was occupied on someone else. She brought up a different topic that grabbed his attention.

"Hey, did you say or do anything to spook Claire?" His eyes shifted from the road to her.

"No, why?"

"I don't know. She seemed kind of weird. Earlier today she came over to talk about you and said that you were acting strange. Whatever it is got her a little worried about you. She thinks you're on drugs," she laughed at the thought. Michael's face was stern. Her smile faded.

"What? Why would she think that?"

"I don't know. I told her you seemed fine to me when we talked this morning. But she went on about not wanting to fire you and hoped that you weren't doing drugs."

"She said that?" his voice upset and hands firmly gripping the leather steering wheel.

"Yeah. I don't why she would be worried about you. She's just crazy. Forget about it."

He turned at her and smiled. "Yeah, there's something wrong with her. Drugs?" he chuckled. "I barely even drink. I think the long years of being alone can greatly affect the emotional stability of a person. Perhaps she's reflecting her own self onto others and is too afraid to admit that she hasn't been right for a while now and is a heavy drinker herself. I've caught of whiff of alcohol in her breath. Tries to hide it with mints, but I have a strong nose."

"Really? I guess I never noticed, but she does say things that are odd so I wouldn't put it past her. Turn left on the next street."

The tires rolled to a slow stop in a front of a white house with its porch light on. They could see the lights on inside from two wide windows on each side of the house. "I wish I could invite you in for a drink or something, but my parents are home and they don't like me bringing boys over."

"No, I get it."

"Well, if you're not in a hurry we can hang out somewhere nearby."

"No, I'm not in a hurry."

He pushed the engine start button and the pitch-black car grumbled. The tires sped off as Gisselle guided him through the backstreets of Alta Park, a neighborhood where the middle class resides. "Just up ahead, passing the house with the white pillars," she said pointing forward.

They arrived at a quiet cul-de-sac. Michael shifted the gear in park and cut the engine then turned off the lights. "Should we hop in the back? It's much more comfortable for talking," he said unfastening his seatbelt.

She removed her seatbelt as well and hopped in the back stretching her leg out then swung it over the headrest, her firm bum wiggling in Michael's face as he watched her crawl and twist to the backseat. He opened his door, pushed the lever down to lower the seat and got in closing the door behind him. He locked the door with his key fob and got comfortable in the back. The light post just yards away from the car illuminated her soft skinned face through the rear windshield. Her straight blonde hair flowed down to her belly button. His eyes shifted from her lustful eyes down to her low top showing her cleavage. She poked her perky breasts outward inviting him in. The night was a cool 70 degrees but their hot bodies and warm breath were fogging up the windows.

A strong desire for her warm flesh came over him as he fixed his eyes on her attractive slender figure. She led his hand down her thigh up to her waist. His hands slithered under her top and dug his fingers into her back pulling her in closer. Her breathing grew heavier with exhilaration. Their magnetic lips slowly pulled together under the glare of the moon that shone through the front windshield. Their lips smacked and tongues slathered each other with warm saliva. The squeaks from the leather seat were the only sound on that silent street. Every house near the rounded end of the dead-end street had its light off. The car swayed with their motions. She opened her legs and lowered herself down on the seat resting her head against the door. He was on top staring at her intently. Thoughts of ripping her neck open flashed through his head. He shut his eyes and blinked them open. Blood oozed out of her neck. Her eyes were rolled back, all white, the lower round part of the iris barely visible just before disappearing behind the eyelid. In terror he blinked them again and at opening them he saw her eyes had been gouged out. Thick blood poured from out of the eye sockets and Michael gasped in terror. The horrible sight pulled him off the corpse and fear held him against the window like a fly stuck on a spider's web. His fingers desperately felt around for the door handle. It wouldn't open after several attempts. He squealed with terror. His other hand fumbled around in his pockets for the key fob. Following a few moments of desperation, he unlocked it and ran out of the car slowly backing away, staring through the driver's side window. Streaks of splattered blood slid down the pane. In the shadows of the yard from the last house on the rounded end of the street, he felt an eerie presence smiling at his torment. Laughing maniacally in the dark under the bark of the tree.

The wind whistled airily and brushed his ear. He felt the cool breeze pass over the small drops of sweat that had formed on his forehead. The whistle then carried with it faint words that danced in the air like a feather. They muttered the words Peter softly in his ear. Rip her apart.

He shook his head trying to eject the words out of his ear like trapped water. The sound of the passenger door handle fidgeting and car door opening stiffened his body. A knot formed in his throat, and he had to remember to breathe. A shadowy figure emerged from inside. The head poked out of the car and it came closer into the light. "What's wrong with you Michael?" Gisselle cried out standing in front of the open door. A look of disbelief came over his face. She was okay. No blood. Her body was intact, and she was alive. Relief washed over him, and he slowly stepped toward his car. "You, you, you're alive," Michael mumbled examining her with his eyes. She came around the car with confused eyes and grabbed his hand. He felt the warmth of her touch and was delighted to feel it. "I think you're not well Michael. Maybe you ought to go home." He stared at her in silence then found his words. "I'm sorry. I don't know what came over me. I'm seeing things that aren't there," he said squeezing her hand. "I just need some sleep is all. I'll take you home now."

The car ride back to her house lasted two minutes but felt like an eternity. Awkward silence sat in the back seat, smiling devilishly during the entirety of the drive as the car cut the streets and made turns.

The car stopped in front of her house and before he could say a word, she had flung open the door. He gently placed his hand on her shoulder and she tensely looked at him with one foot hanging out the door. "I'm really sorry about tonight," he said. She swatted his hand away and stepped out slamming the door behind her. She stopped in midstride and turned around. "Maybe it would help to see a psycholo-gist, Michael. Don't take it in a negative way. Just some friendly advice. Anyway, goodnight." He watched her insert the key, turn the doorknob, and enter the house. At that moment, he felt the vibration of his phone in his pocket. Can we talk? the message read. It was Lilith. His eyes rolled back. Definitely not now. He peeled off leaving black tracks of tire marks on the street.

The next day, Michael showed up to work with dark circles under his eyes from tossing and turning all night but walked in fast paced eager to talk with Gisselle. Maybe she was right. There were unexplainable things going on and seeing a head doctor would be a good thing for him. At entering the store, he crossed eyes with the store supervisor Claire who was shoving a cart into another. She quickly looked away at seeing his disgruntled face and pretended not to see him. Michael kept walking ahead, passing every aisle searching for Gisselle. He walked throughout the large store and searched in the break room. He found Miguel, a short stocky co-worker and asked if he had seen her. He informed her that Claire told him that Gisselle had not shown up to work. The news upset him although he couldn't blame her for not wanting to come in. Last night's psychotic episode was enough to scare her away. At that moment Claire walked in and smiled at him awkwardly. He seized the moment to ask about Gisselle.

"So, I heard Gisselle didn't come in to work?"

"No, she didn't. Maybe she's sick. Strange though. She seemed fine yesterday when I talked to her."

"Yeah strange."

"Did she look sick to you yesterday when she got in your car?"

"What's that?"

"I saw her get in your car last night. I assume you took her home? Did she look okay when you dropped her off?"

"Oh, yeah. She looked fine. Must have been something she ate that made her sick."

"Hmm, yeah maybe."

Claire gazed at him skeptically as he walked away to begin his duties.

During his lunch break, Michael sat in his car with the seat down and eyes shut taking a nap. His eyes darted around as he dreamt. In the dream, he was back at Gisselle's porch in between the two pillars staring at the front wooden door. He heard loud exhalation noises upon entering the residence. The entrance was immediate, and the house was dark. The living room was to the left of the entrance and bedrooms to the right. He moved into a hallway that led to the bedrooms. Loud snoring from a man was heard coming from the first bedroom on the left. Michael walked past it and walked toward the end of the hallway and stopped in front of a white wooden door.

He softly pushed the door open. A bed with a diamond tufted headboard faced the door. Michael fixed his fiery eyes on Gisselle who laid asleep on her side with cell phone beside the pillow. The wall beside her was adorned with hanging string lights.
Michael slipped through the half-open white door, creeping his way toward the bed casting a large shadow over it which grew monstrously as it got closer. The shape of the shadows head was canine in appearance. The mouth stretched out like a snout. Its fingers were long and pointy. Gisselle turned to lay on her back still asleep, pulling the cover over her shoulder unaware of the menacing presence leaning over her. Michael placed his hand over her mouth. The skin on his palm was coarse like leather. The hair on his knuckles that ran down his arm were long and stiff like fur. Gisselle shot her eyes open and widened with terror at the sight of Michael staring down at her. His hand muting her shrieks of horror smelled of musk. She grappled with his stiff arm that pinned her down, but his brute strength overpowered her. She swiped at his face with her hand gracing his lips with her long fingers. He bit into her fingers, cracking the bones as they broke and ripped them off. Thick blood flowed out from her mangled hand. Tears poured from her eyes that splattered onto the pillow. Her muffled cries of pain echoed through the bedroom. She painfully listened to the crunching sound of her fingers being chewed.

He bit down on her belly, tearing off her flesh and began to eat her alive. The wall was splattered with blood which streaked down like dripping paint. Droplets of blood dripped from the hanging string lights. He clamped down on her belly puncturing the skin around her bully button with his long fangs. She thrashed around the blood-soaked sheets trying to free herself from his grip, but his mighty hold was too strong. He lifted her inches off the bed with his mouth and ripped a large chunk of warm meat from her midsection. She huffed loudly under his palm with tears pouring from her eyes and arms flapping wildly. The noise from her struggles and agonizing cries had wakened her father who rushed in through the door. Michael's vicious eyes locked onto Gisselle's father who stood in the middle of the bedroom frozen with terror. The fifty-two-year-old man with greying hair and strong built looked up at the gigantic beast stepping toward him. It's paws in place of feet thundered as it moved forward. Gisselle gurgled blood and gasped for air as she clutched her stomach. Her father lunged at the beast but was quickly overpowered by the immense strength it possessed. He seized his arms and shoved the middle-aged man against the wall. The man's arms were lifted and extended. He let out a painful yell as his bones separated at the shoulder and skin stretched out tearing at the armpit. The beast tore into the man's face sheering the skin off his cheek. The man kept screaming in agony, feeling the pain pulsating through his crippled arms and torn face through his debilitated body. The torture continued through the night as the beast gorged on human flesh from Gisselle's father who moaned with faint breathes as he was eaten alive. Gisselle had bled out from her fatal wound.

At that moment, Michael was wakened from his nightmare by loud knocking on his window. Miguel stood outside the driver's door with work vest clutched in his hand.

Michael rubbed his eyes and rolled the window down. He looked up at Miguel with a woozy face. "Hey man, have you been sleeping this whole time?" Miguel asked.

"What?" asked Michael in a daze.

"You've been gone for three hours."

Michael looked at him strangely then looked out the windshield and saw the sky had turned to a reddish hue. Thin clouds reflected the sunsets red and orange gleam. He realized the sun was beginning to dwindle and he had napped through his work shift.

"Claire was looking for you."

"Fuck. Okay I'll talk to her and tell her something came up and I had to leave in an emergency."

"Too late," Miguel said pointing his eyes at the front door. Claire was walking out and stared at both of them. Michael opened the car door and walked up to Claire. His mind raced to find an excuse. Several of them rushed through his head, but none very credible.

"Sorry for coming back so late," Michael said looking apologetic. "My sister was feeling sick, so I went home to check up on her and had to take her to the hospital."

"Oh my. How's she doing?"

"She's fine. Just has a fever."

"Oh good. I'm glad she's doing fine."

"Should I stay and make up the hours?"

"No, go home. Jaimie is here now, and I can't have two people working the same shift." She walked to her car and stared back at Michael before opening her car door. Michael looked up at the red colored sky and wondered how he could have overslept. First time that ever happened. The most he's ever overslept on a nap was thirty minutes making him late for class. He got back in the car and slammed the door remembering the nightmare. It was horrifying and the vivid gory details caused him anxiety. He put the gear in drive and drove to Gisselle's house to apologize.

He wasn't planning on staying long. He simply wanted to pass by and hopefully see her through the window and say a few words. Stalkerish, he thought, maybe, but seeing her would calm his nerves. He turned onto her street. Flashing red and blue lights illuminated the block. Spinning red lights bounced off the gleam of cars parked in Gisselle's neighborhood. There were three police units stationed in front of her home, a fire truck and ambulance and white coroner truck making its way through the emergency vehicles. Michael quickly got out of his car and flagged a neighbor down who was observing from his lawn.

"What happened?" Michael asked.

"My neighbors were murdered last night," said the man with large belly that dropped below his waist. "Family of three. Heard 'em say it was a massacre. Something straight out of a horror film."

"Dear God." Michael grew visibly panicked. "Who were the victims?"

"A Man, Bill Daniels, his wife Denise and their young daughter Gisselle. Such a tragedy."

Michael crouched and buried his face into his hands then brushed them over his head staring at the house in disbelief. The neighbor looked down at Michael with a somber expression and laid a hand on his shoulder. "Did you know them?" he asked.

Michael looked up at the man with a distressed look in his eyes. "No, no, I don't know them." He got up and went back in his car. The tires screeched as he sped away. He looked up at the rear-view mirror and saw the reflection of the old man from the antique store sitting in the back seat laughing at him, wheezing as the laughter grew louder. Michael slammed on the breaks. The tires squealed to a halt. He turned to look over his shoulder but the old man had vanished. Michael looked all around then rubbed his eyes and looked back at the rear-view mirror. There was nothing. A blue van from the local news station honked and rushed past him toward the house of the recently murdered victims. An unsettling feeling sprang up from his shoulders that crawled to his neck. He felt the strong presence of an entity looking at him. Michaels knuckles tensed as his fingers tightly gripped the steering wheel. Sweat formed under his palms. A tingling feeling from his right ear shot down to his spine. The car engine rumbled and the stainless-steel exhaust pipe vibrated releasing hot gasses into the cold air. His eyes looked up at the rear-view mirror and again saw the figure of a man sitting directly behind him. Dark shadows covered his face.

Michael swiftly turned his head around to look behind his seat and the man had vanished. In his place was the rolled up black leather belt. Michael stared at it with fear as if it were an occult artifact or the culprit for a slew of violent attacks. Which to him, it was and the sole reason for his torment. He picked it up and chucked it out the window.

He sighed, leaned his head back against the headrest and closed his eyes. The weight of his living nightmares buried him deep into depression and set off an anxiety flare-up. Everything was copacetic just a few weeks ago, before that damned belt came into his life. Thenceforth his life started to go to hell and now the possibility of his soul making its way there was real. Hyperventilation set in. Huffs of rapid breathes were accompanied by the sound of his increased heartbeat. The stages of an anxiety attack were in full gear and marching forward like a German blitzkrieg. To combat his disorder and seek some comfort, he sought out help from the one person who always knew how to bring it under control.

Lilith was startled by the loud tapping at her door. She kicked off the throw blanket she was snuggled in and got up from the sofa. She saw Michael through the peep hole looking panicked and in distress. She smirked and opened the door leaving the chain lock secured. Michael took a step forward and bounced backward as if bumping into a force field after seeing the chain blocking his entrance. "Look, I know I haven't responded to your messages or responded your calls, but I've just been going through a lot of shit and right now I could really use your help? So, can you please let me in so we can talk? Please?" He stared at her through the cracked open door with watery sad eyes that told of his pain. Although she was extremely upset with his recent cold behavior, she still loved him and cared for him. She slid the chain lock off and held the door open. He embraced her and broke down crying. She held him, massaging his back as he poured out his emotions. They sat and talked for a long while until the late hours of the night. Michael omitted several details, such as Gisselle and the other mutilated corpse found at the park. She was sympathetic to his troubles and understood that he might be having a mental issue that could progress if not treated soon. Instead of chasing an argument or exacerbate their problems, she let it go and gave him a warm hug.

"An old friend of mine from high school studied psychology in college and is now doing her residency at the UCLA medical center. What if I giver her a call and ask if she could see you? I'm sure she'd be willing to help and not charge you for the consultation."

"You think I'm going crazy?"

"Well, I think you're going through a lot of stress and that can take a toll on someone both mentally and physically. I think it's worth a shot to hear what she has to say. Maybe she can help or prescribe you medicine for your anxiety or something to help you get some sleep, which judging by your dark circles, I'd say you need more of."

"I guess it wouldn't hurt to go talk with her. Okay, I'll do it. Let me know what she says and when she's able to see me."

"I'll give her a call first thing in the morning."

He relaxed and lay his head on her bosom. She caressed his cheek and turned on the television. She turned to the local news channel and news anchor Tom Hoyt was finishing up a report about the third disappearance of a child in over three months. The latest disappearance occurred at Taylor Park where a mother watched her little girl play in the sand and when she turned to check on her nine-month-old baby, the infant was missing from the stroller. She quickly called 911 and local authorities combed through the park but found no traces of the missing child. Authorities are hoping the public will come forward and share any information they may have regarding the abducted child. The Breaking News banner flashed in bold blue letters and Tom Hoyt turned it over to reporter Vivian Pena. Lilith clicked on the remote and skipped the channel.

"Wait, go back," he said sitting up straight with a concerned look. "Go back to the news channel."

The reporter was broadcasting live from the corner of a home that was taped off with yellow tape. The cameraman zoomed in on the coroner carrying out a black body bag and pushing it in the back of their van. Michael intensely focused in on the details of the home. He saw two white pillars and a window on each side of the pillar. He recognized it. Gisselle's house was being covered on the local news.

"Turn it up," he demanded. Lilith pressed the volume up button and shifted her eyes between the television and Michael in a concerning way.

The reporter went on to say:

The mangled bodies of nineteen-year-old Gisselle Daniels, her father Bill Daniels and mother Denise Daniels were discovered by officers who responded to noise complaint. Upon arriving, they found the front door ajar, announced their presence, and entered the residence where they found all three family members deceased. According to authorities, the victims appear to have been mauled by a large animal like that of a bear. Details into the mauling are still being examined. Authorities did make it clear that a homicide is not being ruled out for now due to the nature of their death. An investigation into their death is underway.

Michael looked down at the floor lost in thought. Lilith placed her hand on his shoulder and tugged him.

"Are you okay?" she asked with concern. He faintly heard the question, as if she was off in the distance.

"I'm fine," he replied.

"Did you know them or something?"

"No. It's just such a weird case. Were they killed by an animal or man?"

"Yeah, it's strange. I guess once the detectives continue their investigation, we'll get an answer. But I agree, it's very strange."

Chapter 5

John Milat, a homicide detective for over twenty- years was sitting at his desk sipping black coffee out of a stainless-steel mug his ex-wife gifted him five years ago for his 43rd birthday. He preferred to drink his own premium ground coffee which he purchased online from a Colombian coffee plantation rather than drinking that freeze-dried crap served at the station. Every morning he'd brew himself a cup of that aromatic and tasty coffee leaving his small kitchen in a tiny apartment smelling earthy warm and nutty. The man with large frame and thinning hair on the crown of his head reviewed the autopsy of the Daniels family. All three were bitten by an animal with abnormally large fangs. Larger than that of a mountain lion, wolf, or bear. He continued to read the pathology report noting that the bite marks corresponded to that of an animal, but the bite force corresponded to that of a man. John Milat set the mug on his desk overfilled with folders and paper sheets bound together and sat up straight in his chair intensely reading the report. Humans have an average bite force of 120-140 pounds of pressure per square inch and for comparison a dog has a bite force of 230-250 psi. A mountain lion's bite force is approximately 400 pounds per square inch. The bite force examined on the bodies of the Daniels family were between 120-140 psi. John looked up in astonishment and quickly realized that the Daniels family was murdered. In addition, the width of the bite marks were forty millimeters. The keys from John's keyboard clattered as he searched the web for mouth opening of a human and found that the mouth opening varies from person to person, varying between forty and sixty millimeters further proving that the bite marks from the Daniels family came from a person. John was determined to find the murderer responsible for their death.

The bright morning sun that peeked in through the gaps of the window curtains woke Lilith from her sleep. She lied nude next to Michael who was sleeping on his side and breathing heavily through his nose. He was also naked. Their clothes were scattered in the living room. Socks had been thrown toward the kitchen, bra flung behind Michael's head and landed on the sofa hanging low, black panties were placed over the sofa head. Before going to bed the night before, they reconciled on the sofa.

She got up from the bed to use the bathroom careful not to make a sound and wake Michael. She turned the doorknob gently and quietly pushed the bathroom door closed and flipped the light switch on. She gasped at her reflection in the mirror and quickly locked the door. She stared at herself in the vanity mirror that hung over the sink. The skin on her face was flaky. Bits of hard, dried skin dangled from her cheeks. Pale brown spots marked her face and wrinkle lines stretched down her eyes and traced her forehead. Her eyes were puffy and swollen. A strand of grey hair fell from the top of her head before gently landing in the sink. She combed her fingers through her hair shaggy thick hair and easily pulled out strands of gray hair. She stared down at the locks of gray hair in her palm with panic. Her hands were wrinkled and covered with age marks, like the brown spots over her face. The green veins on the back of her hands were raised and her fingernails had grown long and yellow with darkened cuticles. She held them out in front of her and watched as they trembled, staring at the opaque and unsightly nails. She had aged overnight and looked like an old woman well over a hundred. Her breasts sagged down to her bloated belly. Flaps of wrinkled skin around her stomach hung over each other. The crease from the layers of skinfolds smelled like the inside of a dumpster behind a restaurant that's accumulated the foul stench of alcohol and food waste spilled over the years. She needed to rejuvenate before Michael would wake and find her in her true form. A form that she's kept a secret for centuries. She needed the flesh and blood of a child again to transform back into a young woman.

Jimmy's blue backpack bopped side to side as he walked to school. The box of Crayola crayons inside the front small pocket clacked with every step. His coloring book and children's book about the missing frog shuffled sideways as the curly haired nine-year-old plodded joyfully off to elementary. Today was show and tell at school and he hoped to make friends by impressing them with his favorite book. His father would read it to him when he was younger. His dad had read it to him so many times that he knew it by heart. Could read it back to you word for word without ever looking at the page. The story was of a frog that was taken from his natural habitat and placed in a doctor's office inside of plastic tank decorated with rocks and tiny wood branches. Three days later after several failed attempts, he made a daring escape to return home. Kirby the frog went on several adventures, made lots of new friends along the way and crossed many ponds to finally get back home where all his friends and family rejoiced in his return. Jimmy loved the idea of having an adventure like Kirby the frog and making new friends. Jimmy didn't have any friends and was far from being a popular kid. He was shorter than most kids his age and was picked on for his tiny stature. On the playground, kids would make up teams to play a sport, but Jimmy was almost never picked or if by luck when he was, he'd be the last choice. What will they tease me about today, he thought every night just before going to bed. For that reason, he dreaded going to school and every morning made a fuss. To momentarily escape the dreaded reality of his loner life, he'd imagine going on an exciting adventure as he journeyed through his neighborhood on his way to school, making imaginary friends along the way. In some of his adventures he was a pirate navigating a large wooden ship through the green seas that were his neighbor's lawn in search of a buried chest filled with gold and pearls. Sparrows were Mermaids who sang their hypnotizing song as the ship with a figurehead of a curvy mermaid with long wavy hair crashed through choppy waters. Other days he was a pilot flying a small airplane over uncharted corners of the earth. He made a new friend along the way with every new adventure that guided him to his destination. In his playful imagination, school was the destination of where his journey would end. And for those ten minutes before walking up the three steps that led to the school entrance fitted with large blue doors, he was happy.

He cut through his neighbor's recently mowed lawn for a quick shortcut. As he came around the shrub, he bumped into a figure wearing a tattered black cloak. It faced the driveway staring at a woman fastening a car seat in her Honda RV. Jimmy looked up at the figure and politely apologized. The slow-moving figure turned its head down at Jimmy and snarled. Her grotesque and decayed teeth made his little body tremble with fear. His face went ashen. He took a step back, lost his footing and fell on the grass dampening his blue jeans from the morning dew. The old woman stepped closer, and Jimmy scooted back. His hands were now moist from pushing backward on the wet grass. She snarled again like a feral cat and Jimmy shut his eyes in fear of what was to come next. He put his little hands up to block his face and a second later there was silence. He fearfully opened one eye expecting to see the horrors he imagined waiting in front of him, but the old woman had vanished. He shot open the other eye and looked around. She was gone. He took a big sigh of relief and as he got up to his feet, he heard the faint cry of a woman. He poked his head over the bush, standing on his tippy toes and saw a lady in the driveway frantically calling out for her daughter. "Jane! Jane! Jane!" she cried over and again, louder with each repetition. The lady got on her knees and looked under the van, then hopped inside and searched the rear of the vehicle, then crawled to the front and jumped over the seats to the passenger side shouting her daughter's name. Tears were streaming down her eyes at this point and panic carried the screams for her daughter. Jimmy came around the bush and the hysterical lady with long brown hair locked eyes with him. She quickly opened the door and came around the van. "Hey," she frantically said walking toward him and crouched down to his eye level. "Have you seen a little girl, she's 2 years old, her name is Jane." She was sniffling and wiping the tears from her eyes. Jimmy stood silent, momentarily forgetting the near-death experience he had at the hands of a wicked old woman. "N...no," he said regretfully to the lady who had just lost the little ounce of hope she had left. She let out a mournful cry and her eyes flooded with tears once more. She ran back to van and reached for her purse in the passenger seat and took out her cellphone. She dialed 911 and continued her search, looking around the vehicle and the front porch as the phone rang loudly over the speaker. "Hello," she said anxiously as the operator answered. The distraught mother paced back and forth from the van to the porch explaining the mysterious disappearance of her child to the operator. Jimmy felt bad for the lady and thought perhaps the old woman had something to do with it. He stood by patiently waiting for a pause so he could tell her what he saw. "I looked away for one second to grab the bags off the floor and when I turned back, she was gone," the mother cried into the phone. "I had just fastened the seatbelt to the car seat. It's impossible for her to have crawled out of the car seat, she can't even reach the button to release the seatbelt. Oh God, please you have to help me." Jimmy couldn't find the perfect moment to interrupt and blurted, "I saw an old woman looking at you."

The mother paused in her tracks and got closer to Jimmy. "What did you say hon'?" she asked.

"I said I saw an old woman standing here looking at you and then she saw me and was going to hurt me but then she disappeared."

"Who was this old woman. Where was she?"

"She was right there by the bushes just standing there looking at you. I don't know who she was."

Jimmy went over every detail of the incident with the mother and the operator over the phone, then again when a police officer arrived at the scene. The officer called Jimmy's mother who was driving on the freeway on her way to work. She quickly jumped lanes, made an exit, and turned back around to pick him up. When she arrived, two male detectives wearing navy blue suits and black ties went over the incident with Jimmy and his mother and asked Jimmy several questions. They took Jimmy's report and soon after, a white news van pulled up across the street from where the child was abducted and the camera man along with news reporter stepped out. The reporter directed her camera man into position, and she prepared herself with microphone in hand and cell phone filled with notes on the other. The camera focused and she gave the que. The report would be the day's top story and newspaper article headlines would read Another Child Abducted. Concerned parents began to take note as it was the fourth child abduction in less than three months. The unexplainable way in which the child vanished without a trace added to the growing mystery of each case and caused further panic in the city.

That same night, white candles placed in vintage tapered candle holders illuminated a dark bathroom. Two of the lit candles burned on top of the sink, another 2 burned on top of the toilet seat cover. Lilith stood naked inside her bathtub, drenched in blood. Water flowed out of the showerhead above and wet her body. She ran her hands from her face to the back of her head as the water splashed over her head. She stared halfheartedly at the red water running down the drain in a swirl. Tiny pieces of red meat would gather by the drain before washing down with the rest of the water. She lathered a black sponge with lavender body soap and brushed it down her arms and chest, rubbing it in circles around her perky breasts. She scrubbed down to her smooth legs then rinsed off with hot water. Steam gathered in the warm bathroom clouding the vanity mirror. She opened the shower curtains and stepped out. She grabbed a white towel off the rack and dried herself off then wiped the mirror with her hand and saw her reflection. She was young again. Her skin was radiant and smooth like a baby. Her face was vibrant and glowing. Her body was fit and tight. Her skinfolds were gone, and brown patches had disappeared. Her nails were shiny and healthy. Hair was long and voluminous. She smiled brightly at the mirror and her teeth were pearly white. She blew out the candles and called Michael.

Michael's sister was at home in her room working on an essay for English class when the battery icon on her laptop popped up in yellow. She had only minutes left before the battery died. She quickly reached for her notebook bag and dug around in search for the battery charger when it dawned on her that she forgot it at her friend's house. She texted her friend Sammy to confirm. Sammy quickly replied with a picture of the black charger and a response, yep it's right here.

"Ugh," she sighed out load in frustration. The paper was due tomorrow and driving back to and from her friend's house would be time consuming. Her last alternative, ask Michael to borrow his laptop. She got up from her small desk and walked over to his room. She knocked on his door and he answered the door. "What's up," he said standing in the doorway in an old tee-shirt and black shorts.

"I need to borrow your laptop."

"What's wrong with yours?"

"Mine is about to die and I left the charger at Sammy's."

"Why would you leave it at Sammy's?"

"Not intentionally dork, I forgot it. So, can I borrow your laptop? I have a paper due tomorrow."

"No," he said rudely and shut the door in her face.

"Come on Mike, I need to finish my essay TONIGHT!" She banged on his door.

"Not my problem," he said from behind the door.

"Don't be a jerk. I'll make you pancakes in the morning."

He opened the door with laptop in hand, "just kidding, you don't have to. I was going to let you borrow it anyway, but now that you've offered, I'll take 2 please with a little butter on top."

She smiled and grabbed the laptop. "Fine two. Thank you."

She dashed back to her room, set the laptop on her desk, and inserted the USB and waited for it to load. She clicked on the internet icon and noticed several windows open. She clicked on one out of curiosity. The site was about the life of Peter Stummp. She rapidly scrolled through it. Bedburg, werewolf, serial killer, Germany.

She clicked on another window, and it was a news article regarding the recent murder of the Daniels Family. Another window had information about reincarnation. Another window had YouTube open with a video about reincarnation. She clicked open another window that had information about werewolves. She figured she'd better stop opening all the windows or she would find a weird interest of Michael that she might regret learning. As she began typing her essay, there was something about the recent murdered family that she recalled hearing about on the news. She opened the window again containing the news article about the slain family and read that the teenage daughter had worked at Pricemark, the same place Michael worked at. Huh, I wonder if he knew her. Poor girl, she thought as she read details about her death. She thought nothing more of it and went back to typing her essay.

Elisa woke up at 7am to the alarm set on her phone tucked underneath the pillow. The alarms pulsing sound rattled her ear drums, making every nerve in her body want to smash it to pieces. The eye lids slowly raised, and the room came into focus. She sat up with droopy eyes and dark circles underneath. She had diligently worked all through the night, like a nocturnal beaver chewing down trees for building material to create a dam, she completed her essay a little after four a.m. The three hours of little sleep required a double shot of espresso in her cup of coffee that she would later order at a cafe. Within minutes of waking up, she had showered, dressed, and swiftly combed her unwashed hair. Then grabbed her book bag from the bed and dashed out the living room door, rapidly but with care, walked down the porch steps to the pathway that curved left and led to the driveway where her silver Toyota Camry was stationed and pulled out of there like a bank robber. God was on her side that morning it seemed for all the traffic lights were green and had more than enough time for a quick trip to her local cafe for that much needed caffeine in her system. Upon arrival, God it seemed was in a humorous mood. The drive thru line had, at a glance,

8 or 9 cars long and sluggishly moving forward. She gritted her teeth and scolded the cars in front of her. Of all days, everyone decides today's a good day for some coffee huh. Her eyes rolled in frustration and set them to the radio. She changed the station and got distracted at the car in front of her, its rear back lights turned off and moved up the line. Oh thank God. The lights turned back to red as it stopped again. The radio host Sharla did the hourly news update about trending topics and touched on the latest divorce in Hollywood. The celebrity couple, departed after four years of marriage due to infidelity, which ironically was how they met, while filming together they became close and cheated on their former spouse with each other during production of their film. Sharla then did an update about the mysterious Daniels family death. Sharla went on to talk about the mysterious abduction of baby Jane who was stolen in broad daylight from the car seat of her mother's van. The number of inscrutable abductions has left the community in fear and demanding answers. Grainy home video camera shows the baby in the car seat one second and then vanishes the next. Creepy. Poor baby Jane. The car ahead moved up another space and she slowly let off the break.

Professor Cartwright, a middle-aged man with wavy black and gray hair and thick bottle glasses, sat at his desk reading off the names of his class. Elisa snuck through the door like Tom the cat and plotted in her seat next to her classmate Samantha.

"He didn't call my name yet, did he?" whispered Elisa.

"No, you're safe. So did you finish your paper?" asked Samantha.

"Barely. I finished it close to 4 a.m. I've hardly slept and running on caffeine and adrenaline. Feel like I'm going to crash once this class is over. And you?"

"Yeah I finished it like two days ago. I got an early start on it the weekend Greg and I got into a huge fight, you remember? I distracted myself with the essay."

"What did you guys fight about anyway?"

"We had a nice date planned out and at the last minute he cancels on me saying his friend managed to get an extra ticket for a basketball game that was sold out. I wouldn't have minded so much had it not been for our conflicting schedules. With school and work, our time together is limited and he rather go see a stupid game. And I had a cute outfit that I was looking forward to wearing."

"What was it?"

"It was a cute dress I bought at the mall that go with the shoes he bought me, the one's I sent you a picture of."

"Oh, that's a shame. Well, I'm sure you'll be able to wear it on another occasion."

Professor Cartwright spoke loudly and asked for all his students to turn in their essay. Samantha got up and offered to take up Elisa's paper with hers. Samantha stepped over a backpack and walked down the aisle of desks toward the professor's long table. He smiled up at her freckly thin face as she placed both essays on top of the paper stack, nodded his head, then kept his eyes fixed on her behind as she turned and walked back to her chair. Her long brown hair fixed up in a ponytail bopped off her boney back. She was fair skinned, had a Greek nose with a pair of blue eyes. She wore little make up, ever since her mother taught her how to apply it lightly at a young age. A young man moved his backpack from the side of his chair to other side allowing her to pass freely.

"Thanks," Elisa said scrolling through her Instagram feed.

"Yeah of course," replied Samantha. "Did you hear about another child disappearance."

"I did. It's so awful. I feel so bad for the baby's mother."

"I can't begin to imagine what she must be going through. Not knowing who has your baby. Thinking about its health. Did they feed her. Is she hurt? I would go nuts thinking about all those things."

"The way the baby disappeared is so freaky. Like, how and who could have taken her away so fast and just vanish without a trace."

"I hope they find whoever did it and that the baby is still alive."

"Unless whoever did it already trafficked the poor baby. I heard there's been a significant increase in sex trafficking lately. Could be related."

"I certainly hope not. What kind of sick people would traffic a baby."

"This world is full of psychotic people who are unable to distinguish what's wrong from right and to think that they are out there makes this world a scarier place. People are capable of anything is they possess no moral compass. That's why sometimes I'm afraid to walk alone. Even to walk to my car. That's why I carry this with me everywhere I go," said Elisa holding up her safety keychain set with a pink fur pompom decoration. At first glance, it looks like a normal key chain set, but at a closer look the deceiving key chain is a self-defense kit that includes a sparkly pepper spray, a stun gun in the shape of a cell phone, and a loud alarm disguised as an LED light.

"Oh my god," Samantha chuckled, inspecting every utensil. Where'd you get this?"

"My brother gave it to me as a gift for my birthday. The stun gun really works. We were clowning around with it one day when I accidentally stunned him in the ass with it, he dropped to the floor. I laughed so hard I almost stunned myself with it."

"Oh my gosh, poor Michael. Well, it's a thoughtful gift. He really cares about your safety."

"He does. Couldn't have asked for a better brother."

"Is he still dating that blonde girl?"

"Yeah, he is. Haven't seen her around the house lately though. He usually spends the night at her place. My mom doesn't even bother to ask where he's been anymore, she's used to him coming home days later."

"I hate that parents can be stricter with girls than with boys. Before my brother moved in with his girlfriend, well now fiancé, he would do the same thing. Come home days later, or stay out all hours of the night, oh but if it was me coming home even a minute past my curfew, all hell would break loose; my parents would call a search party, an amber alert, and then ground me for a month once I show up. So unfair."

"It is unfair. It's only right for us to have the same leniency as them. But I get why they're like that though. Boys can better defend themselves than we can."

Samantha grabbed Elisa's key chain off the desk and held it up, "I think you have a better chance at defending yourself than your brother can with this Rambo kit."

After class, the girls went to the food court on campus. The large area of four full-service locations had a line of hungry students at each stand. The Chinese fast-food location had the least and both decided on eating there. They got to the back of the line and carried on with their conversation. Samantha brought up a new topic to discuss, a touchy one that was making headlines in the news and had people divided on the issue.

"How do you feel about abortion being illegal here in our state if they pass the law?" asked Samantha. Elisa was caught by surprise by her question. Elisa felt comfortable talking about everything and anything, but she was a little more reserved when it came to religion and politics. Nevertheless, she had a strong opinion on the matter and didn't mind sharing her thoughts.

"I think a woman should have the choice of whether or not to have a baby and it shouldn't be up to law makers to decide for her," said Elisa with strong confidence in her opinion. Samantha was stricken back by Elisa's response. She thought the contrary and supported the ban on abortion.

"I think it should be illegal for someone to a take life. It is not only criminal, but it also goes against God who has the last word of who gets to live and die." Samantha rolled her eyes. Now they were about to engage in a debate about the two subjects she hated talking about. "So, let's say, God forbid, you go home tonight and some rapist sneaks into your room and sexually abuses you and comes inside of you and impregnates you, you're going to have that rapists child? You would be okay with that?"

"Of course, I would not be okay with being raped."

"No, if he got you pregnant. You would be okay with that?"

"I would be okay with bringing life into this world instead of disposing of it. Then if I ultimately decide that I absolutely cannot bring myself to parent the child, then I have the option of giving it up for adoption and pray that they get a warm and loving home and get the love that I wouldn't be able to give them. That would be the more humane thing to do."

Both moved up the line. "How can you be okay with law makers deciding what you do with your body? That's criminal. It's your body and you should be able to have the choice of aborting."

"Yes, it is your body, but the fetus is the body of another living being and you shouldn't have the right to kill that being."

"A woman shouldn't be obliged to carry the child of a rapist. It's her body and she should decide on what happens to the fetus. And making abortion illegal isn't going to do anything but make it unsafe for a woman to getting a safe abortion. Women who seek to get an abortion may turn to dangerous and illegal measures which puts the lives of more women at risk."

"Uhm, what can I get you?" asked the young girl in black apron behind the glass counter staring awkwardly. Steam rose from the trays of food. Samantha looked down at the options and tapped on the front glass. "What's that?" she pointed down at a food item. "It's our new walnut chicken," replied the girl holding a white foam food container. "Let me just have noodles and the teriyaki chicken, no sauce." The girl quickly packed the food and moved on to Elisa who ordered white rice and beef with broccoli. The girls paid separately and sat at a long table by the window facing the school library.

"I just can't bring myself to take a life which begins the moment sperm enters the egg," said Samantha twirling the noodles with a plastic fork.

"And I can't begin to imagine the government eliminating the rights of women and setting us back decades," retorted Elisa scooping up the rice. Both girls continued with the debate while they ate, stating their argument for and against. At the end of the meal, Elisa jumped on another topic which Samantha happily followed, tired of the ongoing disagreements. "Has Greg called you?" asked Elisa sipping diet coke out of the straw. "Yeah, he called me while we were in line to get the food. Probably wants apologize and come over tonight and talk."

"Are you going to return his call?"

"I don't know, should I?"

"I say you make him wait a little, give him some time to think."

"Maybe I'll text him later just to see what he wants."

"Or text him later after we go to happy hour?"

"Happy hour?"

"Yes, after that long ass paper we turned in, we deserve it."

"Well, I couldn't agree with you more on that. Bertos?"

"Yeah I like that place. They make the best spicy margaritas."

"Yummy. Alright I'll go home and change. So, see you at 5?"

"Yay!"

Chapter 6 The Pocketknife

Michael felt uneasy about all the murders that recently have been taking place especially so close to home. He worried for his sister and his girlfriend. He went in search of something to keep them safe. He drove by Adams Street where there were a lot of small shops, like book stores, gift shops, and other small businesses. As he walked down Adams Street, he stopped in front of a fortune tellers' shop. He felt a force drawing him in as he pushed the door open. The place was dim and smelled of sage. There was a bookshelf filled with books for sale on witchcraft and astronomy. Toward the back was a smaller room blocked off by a beaded curtain. A woman wearing a red lace headscarf appeared and walked toward him.

"Hello," she politely greeted him. "How can I help you?"

"Well, I'm not entirely sure," he hesitated. "I'm looking for something but I don't think you sell it. Not sure why but I was drawn in here."

"Fate," she replied. "It's in your cards." He smirked, dismissing her statement.

"What is it exactly that you're looking for?" she asked.

"Well, I don't know really. You know all those murders that have been happening lately? Well, I want something that'll protect my sister."

"Wait here," she said and turned toward the back room.

The seconds ticked by, each one stretching out like an eternity.

The woman reemerged from the shadows, her silver hair gleaming in the soft candlelight as she moved with an unnerving silence. She glided across the floor, her thin fingers cradling a small, delicate object that seemed to glimmer in the dim light. As she approached Michael, he saw that it was a silver pocketknife, its blade etched with intricate patterns that seemed to dance across its surface. "Something to protect them from the beast," she said, her voice low and husky, as she held out the knife to Michael. He took it, feeling a strange sense of comfort as the cool metal settled into his palm.

As Michael's fingers closed around the pocketknife, the woman's gaze never wavered, her piercing green eyes seeming to bore into his very soul. "I must admit, I've been following the news," she said, her voice low and husky, "and I, too, am afraid of what's been happening in this city." Her words hung in the air, like a challenge, as she paused to let the weight of her statement sink in. "The murders, the brutality... it's as if some ancient evil has awoken, don't you think?" She leaned in closer, her silver hair glinting in the candlelight, her breath whispering against Michael's ear.

The woman's breath was cool against Michael's ear, sending a shiver down his spine as she whispered, "This pocketknife is made of silver, a metal said to be toxic to beasts like the one that lurks within the city." Her words seemed to caress his skin, making the hairs on the back of his neck stand on end. Michael's fingers instinctively tightened around the knife, feeling its weight and balance in his hand. The silver seemed to glow with an otherworldly light in the dim candlelight of the shop, and he could almost feel its power coursing through him.

The woman's gaze lingered on Michael's face, as if searching for a glimmer of understanding. Her eyes seemed to look right though him, as if trying to unravel the tangled threads of his sanity. The air was heavy with tension, thick with the promise of secrets yet to be revealed. She straightened, her movements fluid and deliberate, and named a price for the pocketknife. "Five hundred dollars," she said, her voice dry and detached, "a small price to pay for the safety of those you love." Michael's fingers tightened around the knife, feeling the intricate patterns etched into the blade as he hesitated for a moment, then nodded.

Michael's eyes widened in incredulity as he scoffed at the price, the sound erupting from his throat like a harsh laugh. "Five hundred dollars?" he repeated, his voice laced with disdain. "You've got to be kidding me." He shook his head, his fingers instinctively tightening around the pocketknife as if he might drop it in disgust. The woman's expression remained serene, her features unyielding as she countered his skepticism. "The metal is pure silver," she said, her voice firm but measured, "forged with ancient rituals and imbued with powers that will aid you in your struggle."

"Pretty steep for a knife though," Michael's words hung in the air, his tone dripping with sarcasm as he raised an eyebrow at the woman. She didn't seem the least bit taken aback by his outburst, instead, she let out a low, throaty laugh that sent another shiver down Michael's spine. "I see," she said, her eyes gleaming with amusement. "You think this special pocketknife holds less value?"

Michael's hand hesitated for a moment before reaching into his pocket, his fingers brushing against crumpled bills as he pulled out three hundred dollars. The woman's gaze followed the movement, her eyes lingering on the wad of cash as he placed it on the counter. "That's all I have," he said, his voice laced with a hint of apology, as if the amount was somehow insufficient. The woman's expression remained inscrutable, her features a mask of serene composure. She swiftly picked up the cash, her fingers counting out the bills with a deliberate slowness, the soft rustle of paper the only sound in the heavy silence.

After a moment, she looked up at Michael, her eyes gleaming with a mixture of curiosity and amusement. "Very well," she said, her voice low and pleased. "I will accept your offer of three hundred dollars, but on one condition." Michael raised an eyebrow, his grip on the pocketknife tightening as he waited for her to continue. "I will read your cards, free of charge," she said, her voice soft and measured. "I am curious about you, and I believe your future holds a great deal of intrigue."

Michael hesitated for a moment, his mind racing with the implications of her condition. He had always been skeptical of fortune tellers and card readers, but there was something about this woman that made him feel like she could see right through him. He glanced at the pocketknife still clutched in his hand, feeling a sense of reassurance in its solid weight. If she was trying to scam him, she was certainly going about it in a strange way. "Okay," he said finally, his voice barely above a whisper. "I'll let you read my cards." The woman's face broke into a slow, enigmatic smile. "Excellent choice," she purred, her eyes glinting with amusement.

She took him by the hand, her silver hair cascading down her back like a river of moonlight as she led him through the winding aisles of the shop. The air was thick with the scent of incense and sandalwood, and the flickering candles cast eerie shadows on the walls. Michael's fingers felt a shiver run through them as her cool, pale hand wrapped around his, her long fingers interlocking with his like a vice. He couldn't help but feel a sense of unease as she pulled him deeper into the shop, the dim light seeming to swallow them whole.

As they walked, the air grew thick with an expectant hush, the shadows cast by the flickering candles seeming to deepen and lengthen, like dark tentacles reaching out to snuff out the last vestiges of light. The woman's grip on Michael's hand remained firm, her fingers adorned with silver rings wrapped around his. He could feel her eyes on him, boring into his skin like ice picks, as she led him deeper into the heart of the shop. Finally, they emerged into a small, dimly lit room, the walls of which seemed to press in on them with an almost palpable weight.

As they passed through a curtain of beads, the soft clinking of the polished orbs against each other created a melancholy melody that seemed to echo through the dark room. The air on the other side of the curtain was heavy with the scent of old books and sandalwood, the aroma clinging to Michael's skin like a damp shroud. The woman's grip on his hand remained firm, her hand guiding him through the beaded curtain as if he were a puppet on a string. The room itself was small, the walls lined with shelves that stretched all the way to the ceiling, each one packed tightly with primeval books bound in cracked leather.

She sat him on a chair, its wooden frame creaking softly as he settled into its worn cushion. The sound seemed to echo through the small room, a subtle reminder of the weight of years that bore down upon the age-old tomes that lined the shelves. She moved to sit across from him, her piercing green eyes never once leaving his face. Her movements were deliberate, almost serpentine, as she settled into her own chair, its twin to the one Michael occupied.

The woman's gaze remained fixed on Michael's as she reached out to the small, ornate table that sat between them. The table's surface was adorned with intricate carvings of symbols and runes that seemed to dance in the flickering candlelight, casting eerie shadows on the walls. A deck of cards, bound in a worn leather strap, lay on the table, its edges worn smooth by years of use. The woman's long, slender fingers brushed against the strap, causing it to slide open, revealing the deck's contents. The cards, their faces a deep, rich purple, seemed to glow with an otherworldly light as she began to shuffle them with a soft, whispery rustle.

The woman continued to shuffle the deck, her movements swift and precise. Michael watched as she expertly manipulated the cards, her eyes fixed upon his. He couldn't help but feel a sense of unease as she continued to stare at him, her gaze unwavering and intense. "Now," she said finally, her voice barely above a whisper. "Let's see what the cards have to say about you." She began to lay out the cards in a pattern on the table, her fingers deftly flipping each one over as she placed it in its designated spot.

The woman's fingers moved with a deliberate slowness as she turned over the first card, its face revealed with a soft whisper of cardstock against cardstock. Her piercing green eyes narrowed, her gaze intensifying as she took in the symbol emblazoned on the card's surface. A small, enigmatic smile played on her lips, her eyes never leaving the card as she spoke in a voice that was barely audible over the soft crackle of the candles. "Ah, the Lovers," she murmured, her voice dripping with an air of intrigue. "This is your love card, Michael. It represents the current state of your romantic relationships."

The woman's gaze lingered on the card, her eyes seeming to bore into its surface as if searching for hidden meanings. Her smile grew wider, the corners of her mouth curling upward in a subtle, enigmatic curve. Michael felt a shiver run down his spine as she finally looked up, her piercing green eyes locking onto his with an unnerving intensity. "Ah, Michael," she said, her voice low and hoarse, "you are trouble. The kind of trouble that attracts darkness, that draws it in like a moth to flame." Her words were laced with a subtle warning, a hint of danger that made Michael's skin prickle with unease.

The woman's gaze remained locked on Michael's as she continued to speak, her voice low. "Beware of your girlfriend, Michael. She is not what she seems." Michael's heart skipped a beat as the woman's words sank in. "What do you mean?" he asked, his voice cracking with distress.

Her eyes locked onto his, unblinking and all-knowing, her voice taking on a conspiratorial tone. "Your girlfriend, Lilith, she's not what she seems," she repeated, her words dripping with an air of mystery. "She's been manipulating you, Michael, playing on your deepest desires and fears. You're under her spell, and it's a powerful one." Michael's eyes widened as he felt a shiver run down his spine. He thought back to all the times Lilith had whispered sweet nothings in his ear, making him feel like he was the only person in the world.

The woman's gaze shifted back to the cards, her fingers moving to turn over another one. Michael watched with bated breath as the card flipped, revealing its face. "The Fool," she said, her voice barely above a whisper. "This card represents a new beginning, a fresh start. But it can also represent deception and being fooled." Michael's heart sank as he realized the implication of the card. Had he been fooled? By his girlfriend no less. The woman's words confirmed his worst fears, and he couldn't help but feel a sense of betrayal wash over him.

The woman's fingers hovered over the deck, her eyes seeming to hold a deep sadness as she turned over the next card. The Hangman. Michael's heart sank as he gazed upon the ominous symbol, its dark lines and twisted hangman's noose appearing to leap off the card's surface. Her gaze cut deep. "Ah, the Hangman," she whispered, her voice laced with a hint of warning. "This card often represents sacrifice, or the need to let go of something that's holding you back. But in your case, Michael..." She paused, her eyes narrowing as she studied the card more closely.

She hesitated, her eyes darting between Michael's and the Hangman card, as if reevaluating the verdict. Her grip on the deck of cards tightened, her fingers twitching with an unreadable emotion. The air in the room seemed to vibrate with tension, the candles flickering in tandem with her agitated breathing. Suddenly, her hand jerked, and she drew another card from the deck, its edges fluttering like a dying bird's wings as she flipped it onto the table. "Ah, no," she whispered, her voice tinged with a mixture of surprise and foreboding, "this wasn't supposed to be..."

The woman's eyes widened in alarm, her pupils dilating as she gazed upon the newly drawn card. Her voice was barely audible, a faint whisper that seemed to tremble on the edge of sound. "It's...death," she stammered, her words hanging in the air like a specter. With a jerky motion, she pushed back from the table, her chair scraping against the floor as she rose to her feet. Her gaze remained fixed on Michael, her eyes locked onto his with a desperate intensity. "This wasn't supposed to be," she muttered again, her voice laced with fear.

Michael's heart raced as he felt a chill run through him. "Whose death?" he asked, his voice deep in anxiety, his eyes locked onto the woman's pale face. Her gaze remained fixed on his, her pupils dilated with an unsettling intensity. The woman's mouth opened, but no words came out. She seemed to be struggling to find her voice, her eyes darting back and forth as if searching for an escape from the weight of her own words. The candles on the table violently flickered, forming eerie shadows throughout the small room. Finally, she spoke, her voice barely audible.

"There is darkness inside of you, Michael," she said in a fearful tone. "It's a darkness that threatens to consume you, to destroy everything you hold dear. And if you're not careful, it will." Michael's heart raced as he listened to the woman's words, his mind reeling with shock and confusion. "What do you mean?" he asked, his voice trembling.

The woman's gaze never wavered, her eyes locked onto Michael's as she responded to his urgent question. "The card reading is for you, Michael," she said, her voice low and mysterious. "These cards are your cards, revealing the secrets of your fate. And this..." She paused, her slender finger tracing the outline of the final card, "...this is your death." Michael swallowed the lump in his throat as he felt a cold sweat break out on his forehead. He tried to speak, but his voice caught in his throat. The woman's words hung in the air, like a specter of doom, as she continued to study the card with an intensity that bordered on obsession.

As the weight of the woman's words settled upon him, Michael's face twisted into a grimace, his mind reeling with the ominous prediction. He felt a surge of adrenaline coursing through his veins, his hand instinctively tightening around the silver pocketknife. The cool metal seemed to provide a meager sense of comfort, a tangible reminder of the promise the woman had made to protect his loved ones. He got up from the table, the wooden chair scraping against the floor in protest, and began to walk towards the curtain of beads that separated the dimly lit room from the rest of the shop.

He walked out of the small dark room, the beads of the curtain rattling softly as he pushed through them, like a faint whisper of warning. The woman stood there, her gaze fixed on his retreating back, her eyes burning with an intensity that seemed to sear the air around her. Her slender figure was motionless, her arms hanging loosely at her sides, as if frozen in a moment of dread anticipation. The soft glow of the candles and the flickering shadows on the walls seemed to hold her in a macabre dance, as if the very darkness itself was closing in around her.

As he pushed through the beads, the soft rattle seemed to echo through the shop, a gentle whisper that contrasted with the turmoil brewing inside Michael's mind. He paused for a moment, his hand on the door handle, and looked back at the woman. Her gaze met his, and for an instant, they locked eyes, the air thick with unspoken words. Her expression was a mask of concern, her eyes pleading with him to understand the gravity of the situation. Michael's face twisted into a grimace, a mixture of frustration and fear etched on his features.

As Michael's hand grasped the door handle, the woman's worried expression seemed to crack, her eyes flashing with a hint of desperation. Her lips parted, as if to call out to him, but the words remained frozen on her tongue. The air was heavy with unspoken warnings, the shadows cast by the candles dancing across her face like dark omens. Michael's eyes lingered on hers for a moment, his mind reeling with the weight of her words. The silver pocketknife felt hefty in his pocket, a constant reminder of the darkness growing inside him. With a sense of resolve, he turned the handle and pushed the door open, the bell above it ringing out like a mournful sigh.

Michael raced home in hopes of finding his sister. He planned on giving her the pocketknife for her on safety. Hopefully she'll never have to use it, but you can't be too sure. He then thought of going back to the antique store- the source of all his troubles and the answers to all his worrying questions.

Upon arriving home, Michael found Elisa sitting at the kitchen table. He breathed a sigh of relief and took a seat next to her. "Have you been following the news?" he asked anxiously. "There's a serial killer in our city. And the murders are getting closer and closer to home. I'm really starting to worry about you. It isn't safe out there." His voice dropped to a worrying tone, "or anywhere for that matter." He reached out and took his sister's hand, his eyes with a serious gaze. Elisa stared back at him, her expression a mix of fear and confusion. "Yeah, about that," she said and paused trying to find the right words. "Michael, I've been wanting to talk to you about something," she sat up straight and wiggled in the chair trying to find comfort. "The other day when I returned your laptop and placed it back in your room, I found a pile of dirty clothes in your closet. Some of them looked like they had... blood stains. I didn't think anything of it, but it just seems odd that the girl from the park died on the same day you were there. And another girl who was recently murdered, worked at Pricemark, where you currently work." She paused, studying his reaction.

Michael's eyes widened in surprise, his grip on Elisa's hand tightening as he's caught off guard by her words. He tried to process what she was saying, his mind racing with excuses and explanations, but none of them seemed convincing enough. He felt a cold sweat breaking out on his forehead as he struggled to maintain a calm demeanor. "Wh-what are you talking about, Elisa?" he stammered, trying to feign innocence. But his voice cracked, betraying his nervousness. His eyes darted around the kitchen, searching for a plausible explanation, before finally settling back on Elisa's concerned face. He took a deep breath, trying to calm his racing thoughts, and forced a reassuring smile onto his lips. "The bloody clothes, Elisa... it's just work-related," he said, trying to sound as nonchalant as possible. "I had to clean a broken bottle of ketchup that a customer accidentally dropped, and I must have forgotten to wash my clothes. It's no big deal, really." Elisa's expression remained skeptical, her eyes narrowing slightly as she studied his face. "Ketchup, huh?" she repeated, her voice laced with doubt.

Elisa's eyes seemed to bore into Michael's soul, as if searching for any sign of deception. She leaned in closer, her voice taking on a more serious tone. "Michael, where do you go at night? Are you with Lilith?" She asked the question with a hint of accusation, her eyes never leaving his face. Michael's smile faltered for a moment, before he regained his composure. He shifted uncomfortably in his seat, his eyes darting around the kitchen once more. "Yeah, I'm usually with her," he replied, trying to sound casual. "We like to hang out, watch movies, that kind of thing."

Elisa's eyes seemed to gleam with a knowing intensity as she leaned in closer, her voice taking on a slightly sharper tone. "But just the other day you told me you were having issues with her. So how are you always with her if you're having problems in your relationship?" she asked, her words dripping with a subtle accusation. The air in the kitchen seemed to thicken, heavy with unspoken tension, as Michael's eyes darted around the room once more, searching for an escape from the probing question. Michael's face faltered, his smile crumbling as he struggled to maintain a facade of normalcy. He shifted uncomfortably in his seat, his eyes finally settling on Elisa's, eager for a response. He took a deep breath, trying to steady his nerves. "Lilith and I, we're the breakup to makeup kind of couple," he said, his voice barely above a whisper. "We have our ups and downs, but we always work things out in the end." Elisa's expression remained skeptical, her eyes narrowing slightly as she studied his face. "You've been acting really strange lately, Michael," she said, her voice tied up with concern. "And I worry about you. If there's anything you feel you need to say, trust in me, with whatever it is. I'm your sister. You can count on me, just like I know I can count on you."

Michael's eyes dropped, his gaze drifting down to the table as he fidgeted with his hands. He knew he couldn't keep lying to Elisa, not when she was looking at him with such a mix of fear and concern. He took a deep breath, trying to think of a way to deflect her suspicions without arousing more of them. As he sat there, a sudden surge of protectiveness washed over him, and he reached into his pocket, his fingers closing around the metal of the small pocketknife. He pulled it out, the silver glinting in the kitchen light, and slid it across the table to Elisa. "Take this," he said, his voice low and serious.

Elisa's eyes widened slightly as she picked up the knife, her fingers wrapping around the cool metal handle. "What's this for?" she asked, her voice laced with a mix of curiosity and wariness. Michael's eyes locked onto hers, his gaze intense. "It's made from silver," he said, his voice low, just above a whisper. "I want you to have it, for protection."

His face was serious as he emphasized the importance of the silver blade. "It's durable, Elisa, and can protect you from all sorts of evil," he said, his voice low and stern. "I mean, from the kind of evil that lurks in the shadows, the kind that preys on the innocent." He paused, his eyes scanning the kitchen as if searching for any signs of malevolent presence. "You can't be too careful, Elisa. Not with what's been happening lately specially so close to home." Elisa's eyes widened slightly as she turned the knife over in her hand, the silver glinting in the kitchen light. Elisa's thumb instinctively found the small button on the handle of the knife, and she pressed it, the sound of the blade popping out of its sheath filling the tense silence of the kitchen. The silver shined menacingly in the fluorescent light, casting an eerie glow on the table. Elisa's eyes flicked up to Michael's, a mix of fascination and trepidation reflected in her gaze. She turned the knife over, carefully not to slice her hand on its sharp edges as she examined it from different angles. Michael's eyes never left the knife, his gaze fixed intently on the silver blade as if willing Elisa to understand the significance of the gift. Michael's eyes remained stuck on the knife, his eyes burning with an intensity that made Elisa's skin prickle. "Always carry it with you," he said, his voice filled with urgency. "Don't leave it anywhere, not even for a moment." He leaned forward, his face inches from Elisa's, his breath whispering against her skin. "You never know when you might need it." Elisa felt a sudden shiver run down her spine. She looked at the knife again, "I'll carry it with me," she said as it was understood. "Thank you."

"Never leave home without it and keep it by your side at all times," he replied. As Michael's words hung in the air, he suddenly pushed his chair back, the legs scraping against the tile floor with a jarring screech. Elisa's eyes darted up to his face, her grip on the knife tightening as she sensed a shift in his mood. Michael's eyes, still fixed on hers, seemed to bore into her very soul, as if willing her to understand the unspoken message behind his words. Then, without another word, he turned and walked away, his footsteps echoing through the kitchen as he disappeared into the darkness of the hallway. The sudden silence was oppressive, weighing heavily on Elisa's shoulders as she sat frozen, her heart pounding in her chest as she listened to Michael's retreating footsteps, the knife still clutched in her hand. The sound of his car's exhaust pipe roared loudly outside as he sped off toward the antique store.

She couldn't shake the feeling of unease that had settled over her. She glanced down at the silver blade, the seriousness of Michael's tone still ringing in her ears. She pushed her chair back and stood up, her legs shaky as she made her way to the hallway. With a sense of determination, Elisa passed the living room and made her way to the front door. She grabbed her purse from the hook and slipped out into the cool evening air, the scent of blooming flowers and fresh-cut grass filling her lungs. The sky was a deep shade of indigo, with stars beginning to twinkle like diamonds scattered across the fabric of the universe. Elisa took a deep breath, feeling a sense of resolve wash over her. She needed answers, and she knew just the person to get them from. She walked to her car, parked on the street in front of their house, and slid into the driver's seat.

Elisa's hands moved with a sense of urgency as she inserted the key into the ignition and turned it, the engine roaring to life beneath her. She pulled away from the curb, the tires screeching softly as she accelerated down the street. The lights of the houses and buildings blurred together as she sped towards Lilith's apartment, her mind racing with thoughts of Michael's strange behavior and the ominous pocketknife he had given her. As she drove, the streets seemed to grow darker and more frightening, the shadows cast by the streetlights twisting into sinister shapes on the pavement. Elisa's heart pounded in her chest, her senses on high alert as she navigated the familiar streets with a sense of growing unease.

As Elisa pulled up to Lilith's apartment complex, she scanned the crowded parking lot for an empty space. The dimly lit lot was filled with cars, their shadows cast long and ominous in the fading light of day. Elisa's eyes narrowed as she cruised slowly down the rows, her heart still racing. She finally spotted a vacant space and pulled in, the tires crunching on the gravel beneath. She killed the engine and sat for a moment, collecting her thoughts. The silence was a welcome respite from the turmoil that had been brewing inside her. She took a deep breath and collected herself before stepping out.

Elisa's fingers hovered over the intercom button for a moment. What was she doing here she thought. Was Michael's behavior really that odd? Did it warrant her driving all the way to Lilith's place? Her finger slowly withdrew. Her arm dropping slowly to her side. As she started to take a step back, her intuition was telling her to press the button. Her arm slowly began to raise and she firmly pressed the button, the sound of static filling the air as she waited for Lilith to answer. "Lilith, this is Elisa, Michael's sister," she said, her voice firm but laced with a hint of urgency. "I need to talk to you." The static crackled for a moment, and then Lilith's voice came through, smooth and melodious. "Elisa, hi, what's wrong? You sound upset."

Elisa's voice was mixed with concern and trepidation as she explained, "It's about Michael, Lilith. I need to talk to you about him." The words hung in the air, suspended by the static-filled silence that followed. Elisa's eyes darted towards the entrance of the apartment complex, her mind racing with the events that had transpired just moments before and of Michaels odd behavior. She worried he might pull up any minute and find her there. Was she in the wrong for being there to talk about him behind his back. She cared for him as much as he cared for her. It was only right to do all she can for him no matter what his reaction may be toward her actions. Lilith's response was immediate, her voice dripping with a honey-like sweetness that seemed to calm Elisa's nerves. "About Michael? Come on up, Elisa. We'll talk about whatever is bothering you." The intercom buzzer sounded, a loud, jarring noise that made Elisa's heart skip a beat. She felt a surge of adrenaline as the front gate to the apartment complex creaked open, the sound of its mechanical arm swinging wide to admit her. Elisa's eyes flicked towards the gate, watching as it slowly swung open, its metal bars glinting in the faint light of the setting sun. She felt a sense of trepidation as she walked through the complex. She approached the door to Lilith's apartment, her hand hesitating for a moment before reaching out to knock. The sound of her knuckles rapping against the door seemed loud in the still-ness. A chill crept along her back as she waited for Lilith to answer.

The door creaked open, and Lilith's face appeared in the gap, her features illuminated by the warm glow of the apartment's interior. Her eyes, like two glittering emeralds, locked onto Elisa's, and a soft, enig-matic smile spread across her face. The smile was a gentle, soothing thing.

"Elisa, come in," Lilith said, her voice low and rough, as she stepped aside to allow Elisa to enter. The sound of her voice was like a warm breeze on a summer's day, but oddly Elisa felt a cold tremor ripple through her.

As Elisa stepped across the threshold, Lilith's slender fingers closed around the door handle, her grip tightening as she pulled it shut behind her. The soft click of the latch engaging was a subtle sound, but it seemed to reverberate through the air, like the quiet snapping of a twig. Elisa felt a great disquiet as the door sealed shut, the sudden sense of enclosure making her skin prickle with unease. Lilith's eyes never left Elisa's face as she turned the deadbolt, the metallic rasp of the mech-anism a low, ominous sound that seemed to underscore the tension building between them. Lilith's eyes never wavered from Elisa's as she gestured towards the plush, cream-colored sofa that dominated the liv-ing room. "Please, Elisa, sit," she said, her voice low and soothing, like the caress of warm air at dusk. The sound of her voice seemed to wash over Elisa, calming her frazzled nerves, but only slightly. Elisa's eyes darted towards the sofa, her gaze lingering on the intricate patterns wo-ven into the fabric before she finally moved towards it. As she sat down, the soft cushions enveloped her, cradling her body in a warm, comfort-ing embrace.

As Elisa settled into the sofa, Lilith glided across the room, her move-ments fluid and deliberate, like a dancer navigating a familiar stage. She sank into the armchair opposite Elisa, her fingers curling around the armrests as she leaned back into the cushions. The soft glow of the table lamp beside her cast a warm, golden light on her features, illuminating the delicate curve of her cheekbones and the subtle, enigmatic smile that played on her lips. Lilith's bewitching eyes, locked onto Elisa's, and she leaned forward, her voice low as she asked, "What brings you here, Elisa? You sounded...

...distraught on the intercom," Lilith continued, her words dripping with concern, as she leaned forward, her elbows resting on her knees. Elisa's eyes darted around the room, her gaze lingering on the several lit candles finally coming to rest on Lilith's face. She took a deep breath, the sound of her lungs expanding filling the silence, as she struggled to find the right words.

"Lilith, I'm concerned about Michael's mental well-being. He's been acting so strange these few past days. He hasn't been himself lately. And to make matters worse, I found blood-stained clothes in his room, and then the search history on his laptop, he's been searching for news about the recent murders in Santa Monica, serial killers, werewolves, reincarnation. Just a bunch of weird shit. It just makes me think, well, honestly, I don't know what to think, and I'm scared." Elisa buried her face into her hands in frustration.

Lilith allowed Elisa to go on, her expression never changing. She listened attentively as Elisa recounted her suspicions and fears about Michael. When Elisa finished speaking, Lilith leaned back into the armchair, her eyes narrowing as she watched Elisa. "I see," Lilith said, her voice soft. "I think I know what's going on." Elisa leaned forward, her eyes wide with anticipation. "You do?" Elisa asked wide eyed. Lilith nodded. "Yes, I do," she replied with confidence. "But I'm afraid it's not something that can be easily fixed." Elisa's heart sank.

The bell above the door jingled faintly as Michael stepped inside, the scent of aged parchment and something metallic—like old blood—hung thick in the air. His pulse hammered in his throat as the door creaked shut behind him, sealing him in with the thing that was more than just an old man. The old man's black eyes gleamed like polished obsidian under the flickering gaslight as his yellowed fingernails tapped rhythmically against the counter. "You've been having such...

vivid dreams, haven't you?" he crooned, the scent of sulfur faint beneath his moth-eaten sweater.

Michael's breath hitched as the old man's fingers withdrew from beneath the counter, clutching a small, tarnished mirror. The glass was fogged, as if breathing. "Dreams?" Michael rasped, his throat raw. "More like a living nightmare. They're not just dreams, are they? I wake up covered in—" He stopped himself, but the old man's grin widened, revealing teeth too sharp, too many. "Blood?" asked the old man. "Not yours of course. But you already know this. As you already know the one responsible for the grisly murders. Just like you already know what you are, or rather I should say who you were?"

"Peter Stump," Michael answered quite trepid.

"Reincarnated and in the flesh," the old man murmured, sliding the mirror across the counter. "The real question is... do you know what she is?" Michael's fingers twitched toward the mirror. "Lilith?" The name tasted like poison.

The mirror's surface rippled like black water as Michael's fingers brushed its icy frame. His own reflection wavered—then vanished. In its place, Lilith's face twisted into something ancient, her pupils swallowed the whites of her eyes as she whispered words that made the glass vibrate. The shop's shadows writhe like hanged men twisted in the wind. "Your sweet Lilith," the devil hissed, pressing a rotting fingertip to the glass. It cracked like thin ice, spiderwebbing across Lilith's smirking lips. "You rant and rage cursing me for the gift I have bestowed! But as I recall, it was she that handed you the belt, not I. You walked away from me and she took it from my hands and handed it off to you."

The old man's laughter rasped like a blade dragged over bone as he traced a claw down the mirror's fractured surface. "Oh, you poor, mangled pup," he hummed. The glass shivered violently—now showing Lilith handing Michael the belt.

Michael's vision swam red. The cracked mirror slipped from his fingers, shattering on the floorboards—but the sound was swallowed by the roar of blood in his ears. His hands curled into claws, tendons standing rigid as wire. "You lying rot," he snarled, spittle flying. The shop's walls seemed to pulse inward, breathing with the devil's laughter. The belt around his waist— her betrayal—burned like a brand. The old man didn't flinch. He leaned closer, yellow nails digging into the counter. "Oh, the pup has fangs after all," he whispered.

The devil's grin split wider, the skin at the corners of his mouth cracked like old parchment. His breath curled out in a sulfurous plume as he whispered, "Your rage is wasted on me, little wolf." A gnarled finger rose, pointing toward the shop's grimy window where the neon glow of Santa Monica pulses beyond the glass. "She's out there right now—with your sister."

The devil's finger lingered in the air, its cracked nail glinting like a dagger in the flickering gaslight. Shadows pooled around Michael's feet, slithering up his legs like vines as the old man leaned in, his voice a serpent's hiss, "Lilith is where you ought to be with all that pretty rage, boy," the old man whispered, his cracked lips peeling back from blackened gums. "Before she peels your sister apart just to watch you howl." Michael's breath came in ragged, animal bursts—his fingers twitched toward the belt's buckle, the cursed leather buzzing against his skin. The shop's gas lamps flickered wildly, casting jagged shadows that lunged at the walls like things alive.

Michael lunged for the door, his shoulder slamming into the frame hard enough to splinter wood. The bell shrieked as it tore from its hinge, clattering to the floor like a dying thing. Behind him, the old man's laughter bubbled up like molten lava, thick and choking. "Run, Peter Stumpp!" the old man shouted.

Michael's fingers dug into the doorframe, splinters biting into his flesh as he whipped his head back toward the old man. "This isn't over," Michael snarled, blood from his torn palms smearing the wood. His voice was raw, half-human—the wolf's growl threading through it like barbed wire. "I'll come back for you."

"No need to look hard, wolf of Bedburg," he murmured, his voice suddenly too close, though Michael hadn't seen him move. The stench of scorched sugar and rotting meat filled the air as the old man's shadow stretched unnaturally across the floorboards, twitching like a hanged man's legs. "I'm always around." Michael rushed to his car pulling the door open. He looked back at the antique store one last time and shock settled on his face. The store was boarded up again and all the lights were off. It looked as if though it had been abandoned for years. Michael jumped into the driver's seat and raced off.

As Lilith's words hung in the air, Elisa felt her skin tingle with unease, the sensation spreading like a cold, dark stain through her veins. The dim lighting in the room seemed to grow even more oppressive, the shadows cast by the flickering candles twisting into grotesque, macabre silhouettes on the walls. Lilith's eyes, those unnerving green orbs, seemed to gleam with an otherworldly intensity, as if they were sucking all the light out of the room, leaving only an abyssal darkness that threatened to consume Elisa whole. As the darkness seemed to coalesce around her, Elisa felt her breath catch in her throat, the air thickening into a palpable, suffocating presence that pressed against her skin. Lilith's eyes seemed to be drawing her in, pulling her down into a vortex of malevolent intent that threatened to consume her whole. The shadows on the walls appeared to twist and writhe, like living things, as candles flickered. Lilith's voice, soft and low, seemed to caress Elisa's skin, sending shivers down her spine as she spoke. "You see, Elisa, Michael is... ...a vessel, a conduit for something long-lived and primal, something that has been awakened within him." Lilith's words dripped with an unholy reverence, her eyes gleaming with an otherworldly intensity as she leaned forward, her face inches from Elisa's. The air between them seemed to vibrate with an electric tension. "He has the power now to flood the city with blood and I'll see to it that he does." A slow, serpentine smile curled Lilith's lips as she burst out in laughter. Her breath wafted across Elisa's face, carrying the scent of incense and something else, something sweet and decaying. As the sweet, crumbling scent wafted across Elisa's face, her stomach churned with a growing sense of nausea, the sensation mingling with the fear that had taken up residence in her chest. Lilith's breath seemed to carry a dark, almost palpable energy, one that made Elisa's skin crawl with discomfort. Lilith's eyes seemed to bore into Elisa's very soul, as if searching for something hidden deep within her. As Lilith's gaze continued to bore into her, Elisa felt her very essence begin to unravel, thread by thread, like a tapestry torn asunder by some unseen force. The air between them seemed to thicken, taking on a life of its own, as if the shadows themselves were coalescing into a palpable, malevolent presence. As the darkness seemed to seep into her very pores, Elisa felt her heart racing in her chest, the sound of her own pulse pounding in her ears like a death knell. "You know what, I think it was a mistake coming here," Elisa gently said hiding the tremor behind her words.

With a surge of adrenaline, she slid off the couch, her legs trembling beneath her as she struggled to find her footing on the cold, hardwood floor. The room seemed to spin around her. With a desperate sense of urgency, Elisa turned toward the door, her eyes fixed on the faint sliver of light that seeped in from the hallway beyond. As Elisa's eyes fixed on the sliver of light, a spark of determination ignited within her, illuminating a path through the suffocating darkness that loomed over her. With a newfound sense of purpose, she took a tentative step forward, her footfall echoing through the room like a bell toll. The sound seemed to shatter the spell that had held her transfixed, and the shadows on the walls appeared to recoil, as if wounded by the sudden movement. Lilith's eyes narrowed slightly, her gaze intensifying as she watched Elisa's faltering progress.

As Elisa inched closer to the door with hand stretched out for the door knob, Lilith jumped out of her seat and chased after her. Suddenly, Lilith's body began to shift and contort, her limbs elongating and twisting in ways that seemed impossible for a human. The air in the room seemed to thicken, the shadows deepening and darkening as if they themselves were being drawn into the whirlpool of Lilith's transformation. Lilith's face, once a vision of beauty and innocence, now contorted into a grotesque parody of its former self, her features stretching and elongating like wax in a furnace. Elisa's mind recoiled in horror, her thoughts struggling to comprehend the sheer blasphemy of what she was witnessing. Lilith's face was a twisted map of ancient, leathery skin, each deep wrinkle telling a tale of curses whispered and blood pacts sealed in secret. Her sunken cheeks framed a sharp, protruding nose that hooked like a raven's beak, and beneath her heavy brow, two glowing, icy green eyes pierced through the gloom — lifeless yet hauntingly aware, as if she'd seen centuries rise and fall. Her lips were thin and bloodless, permanently pursed into a scowl that suggested she was always one breath away from muttering something vile. Strands of lifeless, bone-white hair hung in tangled veils around her face, clinging to her weathered skin like cobwebs clinging to a tombstone. But it was her hands that truly betrayed her monstrous nature — elongated, gnarled fingers twisted like roots clawing from the earth. Her skin was dry and cracked, darkened with age and grime, and each fingertip ended in a grotesquely long, yellowed talon, sharp and curved like the claws

of some ancient predator. They clicked softly when she moved, a sound that could chill the bones of even the bravest soul.

Lilith, the witch, was now less a person and more a force — aged, corrupted, and utterly unnatural.

As Elisa's trembling hand reached the door handle, Lilith's long, spindly fingers shot out, grasping Elisa's arm with an unnatural strength. The touch sent a jolt of electricity through Elisa's body, her skin crawling with revulsion as Lilith's grip tightened, holding her in place. Elisa's arm felt like it was being crushed beneath an unseen weight, the pressure building to a crescendo that threatened to shatter her very bones. Lilith's macabre grin seemed to grow wider, her eyes blazing with an intensity that made Elisa's skin crawl. The air in the room appeared to ripple and distort, as if reality itself was being warped by the sheer malevolence emanating from her. The candles violently flickered, their flames trembling in the faint breeze stirred by Lilith's movements, and the shadows swayed from side to side.

Elisa's body instinctively recoiled, her muscles tensing in a desperate bid for freedom. With a surge of adrenaline, she struggled to free herself from Lilith's grasp, her arm twisting in a futile attempt to break the witch's unnatural hold. Her skin felt like it was being seared by an invisible flame, the heat emanating from Lilith's grasp like a palpable force that threatened to consume her very soul. Lilith's body convulsed, her chest heaving with a malevolent glee, and she let out an evil laugh. A frozen tremor gripped Elisa's spine. The sound was like a rusty gate scraping against concrete, a harsh, grating noise that seemed to shred the very fabric of reality. As the evil laugh echoed through the room, Elisa fought to free herself but Lilith's grip tightened even more. Her long fingers digging deeper into her skin like talons, and Elisa felt a searing pain as if her skin was being flayed alive.

With a surge of desperation, she reached with her free hand inside her pocket and pulled out the pocket knife that Michael had given her moments ago. Its cold metal a comforting weight in her palm. Her fingers wrapped around the knife's handle, her thumb instinctively finding the small indentation that marked the blade's release. With a swift, economical motion, Elisa pressed the indentation, and the blade sprang open, its sharp edge glinting in the dim light.

She cocked her arm and thrust the silver blade into Lilith's neck. The sound of the knife piercing flesh was like a soft, wet crunch, and Elisa felt a jolt of revulsion as she realized what she had done. Lilith's eyes widened in surprise, her gaze locking onto Elisa's as a crimson rivulet began to trickle from the wound, tracing a sinuous path down her neck and onto her shoulder. As the blood flowed, Lilith's grip on Elisa's arm faltered, her long fingers relaxing their hold as her body began to slump forward. She dropped to her knees before slumping forward. Her head lolled to one side. The sound of her labored breathing filled the air, a harsh, rasping noise that seemed to grate against Elisa's eardrums. Elisa's hand, still clutching the pocket knife, felt heavy and unresponsive, as if it had developed a life of its own. The blade, still buried in Lilith's neck, seemed to vibrate with a malevolent energy, as if it was drinking in the witch's life force.

But then, just as suddenly as it had all begun, the darkness began to recede, the shadows retreating back to their corners as a faint, silvery light began to fill the room. Elisa slowly pulled the knife out and watched in stunned silence as Lilith's body began to transform yet again. Lilith's body underwent a transformation that was both mesmerizing and terrifying. Her skin, once smooth and unblemished, dwindled to rotten flesh and bone. Elisa watched in horror as Lilith's face, once a vision of beauty and cunning, became that of an ancient mummy. The eyes, once bright and piercing, darkened and clouded, like two stones submerged in a stagnant pool.

As the last remnants of life flickered out of her body, Lilith's chest rose and fell in a final, desperate gasp for air. Her mouth, now a

twisted, lipless slit, opened wide, revealing yellowed teeth stained with the remnants of dark magic. The sound of her labored breathing, slowed to a mere whisper, a soft, mournful sigh that seemed to carry on the wind.

The door burst open with a splintering crack, and Michael stood frozen in the threshold, his pupils dilating as they darted between Elisa's bloodied knife and Lilith's withered corpse. The air curdled with the metallic stench of blood and something older—burnt herbs and rotting parchment, the remnants of Lilith's dark rituals. Elisa's breath hitched as her brother took a single, shuddering step forward. His fingers twitched at his sides, nails digging into his palms hard enough to draw thin crescents of blood. The black belt around his waist seemed to pulse, the leather writhing like a living thing against his shirt.

Michael's hands flew to the belt buckle, fingers fumbling against the writhing leather as if it burned him. With a ragged gasp, he tore it free, the cursed thing hitting the floor with a wet thud—alive, squirming like a severed limb. Before Elisa could react, he held her against his chest, his heartbeat a frantic drum against her ear. The knife slipped from her numb fingers, clattering beside Lilith's corpse. Elisa's body shuddered against Michael's chest, hot tears soaking through the fabric of his shirt. Her fingers clutched at his back, nails digging in like she might drown if she let go. Michael exhaled sharply—half sob, half gasp—as his hands moved in slow circles between her shoulder blades, the way their mother used to when nightmares woke them as children. "Look at me," Michael said in a low voice. Elisa pulled back just enough to meet his gaze—his pupils still blown wide, the gold-flecked irises shimmering with unshed tears. His thumbs brushed the wet trails on her cheeks, smearing blood—Lilith's blood—across her skin in rust-colored streaks. "It's okay," he murmured, the words cracking like dry earth. "You did what you had to do." A shuddering breath escaped her as she clutched his wrists, feeling the rabbit-quick pulse beneath his skin. She let out a loud cry followed by a river of tears. He wrapped his arms around her once more in comfort as she apologized for her actions. "I'm sorry," she cried barely able to form the words. "It's okay," he reassured her.

Michael's grip on her shoulders loosened slightly as he stepped back, his fingers trembling. His gaze flicked down to the knife glinting on the floor, its blade smeared black-red in the flickering candlelight. He knelt slowly, the floorboards creaking under his weight, and picked it up with deliberate care. The handle was slick—part sweat, part blood—as he folded the blade back into its casing with a soft, metallic click. The sound seemed to snap something in the air. The last of the candles guttered, plunging the room into near-darkness save for the sickly glow of streetlights bleeding through the windows.

Two plainclothes detectives—John Milat and Harris—flanked the door outside of Lilith's apartment, guns drawn. Behind them, uniformed officers stacked up, silent, focused. One of them raised a hand and counted down with his fingers.

3... 2... 1...

BOOM. The door shuddered under the first battering ram strike. Wood splintered, hinges screamed. The door exploded inward with a splintering crack. Officers surged in, boots thundering, voices shouting over each other. "Police!" they yelled. "Hands where we can see them! Down! Get down!" The apartment exploded into chaos. Michael jolted, confused and wild-eyed. He pulled Elisa back out of harm's way and made a quick move toward the kitchen, toward the window. Detective Harris tackled him mid-step, slamming him to the ground.

"Don't even think about it!" Harris roared digging his knee into Michales back while the other officers swarmed on top. The detective's grip was iron around Michael's wrist as he wrenched his arms behind his back. Michael thrashed as cold metal bit into his skin-handcuffs clicking shut with a sound like a bone snapping. Elisa backed away, frozen, her hands in the air. One of the officers grabbed her gently but firmly. "Miss, come with me," an officer with a thick mustache calmly told her. "Keep your hands visible." Elisa stammered, completely shocked.

"What—what's going on?" Elisa asked. "Why are you arresting him?"

"We can tell you about it at the station," replied Detective Milat leading her out the door. Elisa jerked against the detective's hold.

Michael looked up, lip bleeding from the scuffle. His eyes met Elisa.

Michael's shout tore through the chaos, raw and ragged. "Elisa didn't do anything!" Michael cried out. "Let her go! I'm the one you're looking for."

The detective along with an officer's help pulled Michael up by his arms. The officer's voice was a graveled monotone as he marched Michael toward the broken apartment door, each word of the Miranda rights hitting like another cuff around his throat. "You have the right to remain silent—" Michael's foot caught on a warped floorboard, causing him to lose balance. He stumbled, only to be yanked upright by the chain between his cuffs, the metal teeth biting fresh welts into his wrists. Blood from his torn palms smeared the precinct car's door frame as they shoved him inside.

The precinct fluorescents buzzed like wasps as they marched Elisa down the linoleum hallway. An officer's grip bit into her bicep, steering her into a windowless room where the air tasted of stale cigarettes and bleach. She gasped as her arms dropped—dead weight swinging toward bruised hips. The bright bulb above flickered once, twice, casting strobing shadows across the steel table bolted to the floor. "Sit." The detective's command left no room for protest, his index finger jabbing toward the cold steel chair. Elisa's knees hit the seat edge hard enough to rattle her teeth.

"You understand why you're here, Miss Adler." Not a question. Detective Milat's voice scraped against her eardrums; the words laced with something darker than accusation. Elisa's tongue stuck to the roof of her mouth.

The detective's finger thrust toward a manila folder, its edges frayed from use. "We have evidence against Michael Adler, your bother. Our investigation has shown that he was involved in the murders of Jenny Auster and the Daniels family. Your brother left teeth marks in Gisselle Daniel's femur." The file slapped against the table, spilling crime scene photos—grainy flashes of her bedroom wall painted in arterial streaks. "We pulled his hair from Jenny Auster's fingernails. Found his shoeprints in brain matter. He leaned in closer and lowered his voice to a whisper. "He didn't just kill them, Miss Adler." His knuckles whitened around the edge of the photo, the paper wrinkling like dead flesh. "No, your brother did more than just murder those people—he ate them." Elisa's breath hitched—a wet, strangled sound. The chair legs screeched against linoleum as she recoiled, her spine pressing into the cold metal backrest. "Oh God," she cried out in revulsion. Detective Milat leaned back in his chair, arms folded – less aggressive now more analytical.

"Elisa, I need you to understand what we're dealing with here. Your brother didn't just snap. This didn't come out of nowhere."

"What are you saying?" Elisa asked sniffing and wiping her tears.

Milat glanced at a file on the table. Inside was a psychiatric intake form. "We had him evaluated. Preliminary psych says he's exhibiting signs of something rare; Clinical lycanthropy. Ever heard of it?" Elisa furrowed her brow, confused. "Like werewolves?" she asked.

"It's a delusional disorder," Milat explained. "People genuinely believe they're turning into animals. A wolf in his case. It's not just fantasy – it's a break from reality. Violent breaks, sometimes."

Elisa looked like she had been punched in the gut. "Michael thinks he's a werewolf?" she asked with an incredulous stare.

"It appears so. At least while committing these crimes, he believes to be one. This unshakable belief often involves hallucinations and behavioral changes. His delusion is what makes him so dangerous which is why Michael cannot be out there roaming freely," Milat said.

Elisa's fingers laced tightly in her lap. Her eyes flicked between the detective and the manila folder. What he's saying is impossible. "I don't-" Her voice cracked, the words dissolving into another shuddering gasp. The light above flickered. Elisa's fingers trembled against the table's edge. Milat's hand slid across the photos, rearranging them with deliberate slowness – a severed hand here, a gnawed ribcage there – until they formed a grotesque mosaic in front of her.

"You don't what, Miss Adler?"

"It's hard for me to believe this. He's not a monster. I know him. He's got a good heart."

"We're not saying he is. But we can't ignore what he's done. Four people are dead. Maybe more that we don't know of yet. And a whole lot more will end up like these poor souls in the pictures if he gets to walk away." The detective leaned forward, calm and measured.

"Elisa... we need him to talk. We need to know if there are more victims. We need him to confess his crimes. Will you help us talk to him?"

Elisa looked away and contemplated on the chance of seeing her brother again and talk with him. "When can I speak to him?" she asked.

Across the precinct, Michael's wrists burned beneath the steel cuffs bolted to the interrogation table. The air smelled of sweat and industrial cleaner, undercut by something fainter—rust, maybe, or old blood trapped in the grooves of the floor tiles. His knee bounced uncontrollably, the chain between his ankles rattling like a specter's whisper.

The interrogation room door burst open with a pneumatic hiss. A burly man in a rumpled trench coat shouldered his way inside, dragging a steel chair behind him—its legs shrieked against the linoleum like a wounded animal. The newcomer dropped into the chair with a grunt, the metal frame groaning under his weight. His knuckles were split, the scabs glistening under the fluorescent fixtures as he tossed a black sack on the table. Michael stared at him mysteriously.

The detective's breath smelled of stale coffee and nicotine as he leaned in, his knuckles pressing into the table hard enough to blanch the scar tissue. "Listen close, kid," he growled, untying the noose on the sack. "Your sister's next door spilling her guts. The other detective she's with, Milat, he's using her to get to you. Soon, she'll pop in here and ask you to cooperate and play nice with them. And then, you wanna know what's coming? Life behind bars without the possibility of parole. You'll never see the light of day again," he chuckled and shook his head.

The detective's lips peeled back from nicotine-stained teeth in what might've been a smile. He reached inside the sack and pulled out the black belt. He stared at Michael with a devilish grin.

The detective's pupils swallowed the fluorescent light whole, leaving twin voids that pulsed with the rhythm of a slowing heart.

Michael's breath seized in his throat. He looked down in horror. His eyes locked on the belt laid out across the table like a coiled serpent. The silver buckle glinted with a dull light. Michael could feel it humming with that same low, ancient energy that had ripped his soul apart. His breath came in ragged gasps as he stared at the motionless belt. The lights above them popped one by one in showers of glass, each burst leaving behind a greasy afterimage burned into Michael's retinas—the silhouette of horns. The edge of the room pulsed inward, the darkness breathing like a great beast. Michaels chains between his ankles snapped and the cuffs on his wrist unlocked.

The detective's fingers twitched against the table, his nails lengthening into curved yellow talons that scraped grooves into the steel. His black, bottomless eyes shimmered with something ancient and cruel.

"Who are you?" asked Michael with a tremble in his voice.

"Who am I?" the detective's voice unraveled into layered whispers-a chorus of dying men speaking through his rupturing throat. His breath reeking of opened graves.

Michael's vision swam as the detectives face peeled away in strips-not skin, but parchment thin layers of something older, something that smelled of turned earth and spoiled milk. Behind the peeling mask, yellowed flesh sagged into a familiar topography of wrinkles-the bulbous nose, the frizzy white hair, each strand coiling like smoke from a dying fire, stiff with centuries of grime and unnatural preservation, and those piercing black eyes that had watched him from the shadows of the antique store. Michael shoved his chair back with a screech, toppling to the floor. He crawled backward, eyes wide with primal terror, sweat pouring down his neck. He looked around for the door, but the room had collapsed into shadow.

The detective, now revealed to be the old man from the antique store, leaned forward, his lips parted, revealing blackened gums studded with teeth filed to points—each one whispering in a language that slithered into Michael's ears like maggots burrowing into rot. His tongue—blackened and forked—slithered over his sharp teeth as he spoke. "You wore the belt," the devil hissed. "You let me in and now you can't be free of me. Yet, you disappoint me. You've worn my gift poorly, Peter Stumpp." His words congealed in the air, each syllable sprouting legs that skittered across Michael's sweat-slicked skin. "I gave you the power of a hundred men yet you allow yourself be trapped in here like a caged animal. Ironic is not? An animal." The old man's laughter bubbled up like tar through his ruined throat.

Michael cowered against the cold concrete wall, his chest heaving as the old man stood up towering over him.

"You were never meant to be tamed, Michael," the old man said, grinning with cracked lips.

He then reached out and placed the belt on the floor between them. The belts surface was covered in wolf etchings that pulsed with a dark, living glow.

Michael's eyes widened, heart pounding in his ears. "Why have you brought it here?"

"I brought you your freedom," the old man hissed, voice coiling like smoke around the room. "Put it on, and the chains of men will fall away. No more guilt. No more weakness. Just power. The power to free yourself from here."

Michael shook his head violently. "No, I—I don't want this. I've seen what it does. I hurt people—"

"They hurt you first," the old man interrupted, eyes narrowing. "They locked you in a cage. They'll let you rot. But I can make you whole again. Put on the belt... and you'll never answer to them again. Not judges. Not guards. Not gods."

Michael stared at the belt like it was a serpent waiting to strike — part of him repulsed, the other part aching with a primal hunger.

"Use the belt," the old man said, voice dropping to a whisper that throbbed inside Michael's skull. "Become what you were always meant to be. Free yourself."

And in that moment, as the room trembled and the lights above flickered again, Michael didn't know if the fear in his heart was from the Devil... or from the part of himself that wanted to say yes.

Michael stared at the belt, breath ragged, sweat dripping from his brow and pooling at his collar. The Devil's words still echoed in his skull — "Free yourself."

Then, without warning, the lights flickered again — violently this time — casting the room in rapid flashes of light and shadow, like a stuttering film reel on the brink of tearing.

A low, guttural chuckle vibrated through the air, and the temperature dropped.

Michael looked up — but the old man was no longer standing over him. The moment the old man vanished, the interrogation room lights flickered back to life with a sickly yellow glow.

Then... silence. The only sign the Devil had ever been there was the belt lying on the ground, perfectly centered between Michael's feet. Its antiquated leather seemed to pulse faintly, like it was waiting. Michael backed away, heart thundering in his chest. His lips trembled as he whispered, "No... no, this isn't real..."

But he could still feel it — that darkness he thought he'd buried — stirring inside him again. The Devil was gone. But the offer remained. Michael stared at the belt as if it were a living thing — coiled on the floor, humming with dark energy, pulsing in time with his heartbeat. It had once made him powerful. Savage. Unstoppable. But it had also made him something else — something he couldn't live with. He knelt beside it, trembling fingers brushing over the cracked leather. The runes were still warm, still whispering to him in a tongue he didn't understand but somehow felt. Promises of freedom. Strength. Release. But not the kind he wanted anymore.

"I won't hurt anyone else," he muttered, voice barely audible. "I won't become that thing again."

Tears welled in his eyes. The images wouldn't stop — the torn flesh, the screams, the blood-soaked ground beneath his feet. The memory of their faces. The people he loved. Flashes of Elisa. The people he destroyed. Flashes of The Daniels family, his victims. He stood slowly, belt in hand, and looked at the exposed pipe running along the ceiling of the small room — once an interrogation room, now a cage of his own making. He fashioned a loop. The leather was stiff, but it bent. His hands moved with grim certainty. Not out of rage. Not even out of fear. But out of a crushing, inescapable sorrow.

"This ends with me," he whispered. He climbed onto the metal chair, the belt around his neck, eyes staring into nothing. As he prepared to step off, the air around him shifted again — a faint heat brushing his skin. Then a voice — not from the room, but from inside his own mind — smooth, amused, and waiting: "You think death will free you? I offered you freedom."

Michael froze. Every part of him screaming to finish it.

"Go on," the Devil cooed. "But when you hang... you hang as mine," his final words clung to the air like cobwebs. Michael clenched his jaw, fury rising one last time — but not at the Devil.

At himself. God, please forgive me and have pity on my soul.

Then he stepped off the chair.

And the world went silent.

THE DEVIL'S BELT